JACK R. SPARACINO

DANCING

With the

DEVIL

*The Southern Ladies Mafia
Strikes Back*

To order additional copies of this book, contact:
Xlibris
844-714-8691
www.Xlibris.com
Orders@Xlibris.com

ISBN: Softcover   978-1-6641-9348-2
        Hardcover   978-1-6641-9359-8
        EBook   978-1-6641-9349-9

Print information available on the last page

Rev. date: 09/01/2021

Contents

QUINCY BOYS

Billy O'Connell came from a skin tight neighborhood in Quincy, Massachusetts. Money was tight for most families. They tended to grind away at low wage jobs in retail, sanitation, loading docks or Boston area factories. Warehouses. Jobs where you took a shower after work, not before. The kids often showed up at school in tight clothes, hand me downs they had outgrown, but there usually wasn't enough cash left after paying the bills to afford new ones. Most families hesitated to prowl the Goodwill or other thrift stores out of stubborn Irish or Italian pride. Tag sales were rare as caviar at church in most places since hardly anyone planned to move out. This was home. They were oysters cemented to their beds. Glued to their fates before God. Most of them wouldn't move out if they won the lottery, and Lord knows they tried. Discarded scratch tickets littered the sidewalks. You can't win if you don't play.

Billy was pushing eighty and all those years etched his tanned face and hitched his gait. He was still getting around alright, dressed pretty well, often in jeans and a Red Sox hat, and liked to wear jewelry. Gold neck chains, guy bracelets, expensive watches. He sold his Rolex swiped from a jewelry store forty years ago. He smiled and squinted into the sun at Marina Bay in Quincy, even when it stayed hidden behind cloud cover. If you asked who exactly swiped the watch, he always grinned and said "The cops never really knew." Further conversation, once someone gained his trust, revealed that he did hard time after the watch incident, which included two fox coats, five grand in cash, and an entire box of glam jewelry. Stabbing the Asian husband and wife owners repeatedly didn't do him any good, though they both survived before escaping to San Diego and starting fresh. They never forgot that punk. That damned Mick.

Billy and his old buddies liked to hang out at the Irish Pub on Hancock Street. The Irish Pub was one of the best if slightly seedy dive bars in town. It opened Monday through Saturday at eight a.m. Sundays not until ten o'clock per Massachusetts law. The bar tenders were all pals with Billy and his gang, along with the other regulars. All white guys, almost no unaccompanied women. Mostly working stiffs and retirees. A few unemployed. The beer was cheap, the shots generous, the food surprisingly good and inexpensive. Generous portions, like their steak tips with vegetables and mashed potatoes, welcome after a half dozen drafts of Bud or a fistful of Sam Adams (not much call for Heineken or Saint Pauley Girl and the like). Five TV's hung over the bar, usually tuned to sports channels. Just inside the entrance stood a waist high, poorly lit money machine. Handy, since the joint only took cash. Most of the time it actually worked.

Billy's buddies had known each other for over sixty years. All of them grew up together in Quincy. Max and Freddy knew Billy from their time in Souza-Baranowski Correctional Center (SBCC), a maximum security prison in Lancaster, Massachusetts.

Max was overweight and red-faced with a snarled mess of bulging veins crawling over his hard drinker's nose. His square head was sparsely covered with mostly gray hair engulfing a few red strands threaded in. He graduated from Quincy High School on Coddington Street but only barely, seeming to spend most of his time in the principal's office for "disciplinary issues." This amounted to harassing his classmates in the halls while they were fishing things out of their lockers and in gym class. He was a genuine pain in the ass, but somehow likable underneath the rough exterior. In his senior year he was voted least likely to succeed. It pissed him off for the rest of his life. Every time he mugged an old lady he felt a little better about himself.

Freddy O'Brien was always a slightly odd duck. Medium height and build, he was borderline handsome with even features and curly brown hair, now mostly grey, framing deep blue Mediterranean eyes. His chin had a slight cleft which some of the girls found attractive. He tended to stutter around strangers and often peed himself when arguing. Freddie did pretty well in high school. He got mostly B's and excelled in football despite his modest size. What he lacked in bulk and speed he made up for with grit and ferocity, including an occasional kidney punch to an opposing player. The refs always seemed to be looking the other way. Or maybe they just thought hey, that's football. Rough sport. Let 'em play. We got hospitals.

John was the quiet one of the bunch. Tall and still drill bit thin after 68 years. Kids in his school days said he was built like a stick and the nickname stuck. Stick Mulligan. After high school almost no one knew his real name was John and after a while he started ignoring their ignorance about him. He went to trade school for a while and took odd jobs as a welder, electrician's assistant, carpenter and plumber. At twenty-six he started a building company with his friend Ted Stone. They called it Sticks and Stones.

Carl and Mike were brothers. They shared a last name, MacArthur, but not much else besides their working class parents. Carl was the brains of the two. He aced his way through Quincy High and then studied at the University of Massachusetts. He tried majoring in art with an eye on a career in architecture someday but began stealing whatever he could get his hands on to make enough money to pay tuition and sustain his burgeoning life style. One day he got caught lifting a Monet from the Isabella Stewart Gardner Museum in Boston. With several priors on his record he landed a six year sentence. Nobody ever kicked his ass. Before prison.

Mike MacArthur was what people called a dunce. Yet another redhead in a school swimming in them, he barely made it through his sophomore year at Quincy and dropped out at sixteen. He worked in his father's butcher shop hosing down bloody tables and floors for two years and then a shoe factory on light maintenance before being clipped by the police for burglary at neighborhood apartments. One of his "customers" was an undercover cop with a service revolver. Mike figured he lucked out when he drew Billy as his cellmate.

BEER BOTTLE BLUES

Saturday two o'clock in the afternoon. As usual, the wind blasted down Billings Road right outside the Irish Pub. Chicago is called the windy city, but the average wind speed in Boston is actually slightly higher. Billy's entire crew, now well along the straight and narrow professionally or just plain retired, sat hunched over their draft Buds and Sam Adams bottles alongside Wild Turkey shots at the long bar and one of the four-seater tables adjacent. They were all modestly content, solvent, and still in passable health. Sam Winters tended bar for them and the other eighteen customers. Three TV's were tuned to the Patriots game. The Pats were playing Green Bay, the score tied at 10 in the second quarter. Tom Brady was calling the offense for New England as they squared off at Lambeau Field. A plate of fries under a lava slide of ketchup sat on the table, two rare bacon cheese burgers with lettuce, tomato and red onion at the bar.

They all sat quietly while Brady called a third and ten play at Green Bay's forty yard line. Brady dropped back after the snap and faked right before hitting Ron "Gronk" Gronkowski" for a TD pass that the Packers never saw coming. He crossed into the end zone, all 6'6" and 265 pounds of him with no defender within five yards. Billy's gang sprang to their feet and high fived each other and anyone else within reach. The bar rocked like it was glued to Brazilian soccer after a game winning goal. Pandemonium. *Drinks on the house* they shouted.

"Game ain't over yet, boys" Sam growled from behind the bar. "But I ain't heartless," he said reaching for a three quarters full bottle of Wild Turkey and inviting them to pass it around. "Here, have at it. Go Tom!"

Billy and the boys had just settled back into their seats, the whiskey still burning the backs of their throats, when two drop dead stunning women strolled in off the street. Cracking necks could be heard bouncing off the walls as the ladies looked around for a table or booth.

Carla "String Bean" D'Andrea, an attorney by trade, was the drop dead gorgeous forty-nine year old ring leader of a team of six women from Charleston who managed to pillage and plunder much of the city in their twenties and thirties in their search for riches and thrills. They often talked about the pure adrenaline rush they got when robbing banks, jewelry stores and even art auctions. Carla's wing woman was a highly skilled and touted artist, Joanna Ciampa. Although Carla's leggy five foot nine figure dwarfed her in sheer height, not to mention her cover girl looks—complete with dazzling green eyes that brought men to their knees and often rendered them speechless—Joanna was nobody's slouch. Cat 3 hurricane cute and no second banana to the customers and managers she pulverized.

The ladies waltzed over to an empty booth and slid in. Their purses were deliberately modest, so as not to call attention to the weapons they carried. Carla sported a Sig Sauer P226 MK25, the same overpowering model used by US Navy Seals. Joanna carried a Magnum Research Desert Eagle, quite possibly the most powerful handgun available in a semi-automatic pistol. She loved the gun's handling and specs, including 35,000 psi of pressure in the barrel's chamber.

Both ladies also carried knives. Not just any cutlery, these Jagdkommando Tri- Daggers were among the most deadly available. Carla also carried a Gerber LHR combat knife with a 6.87 inch fixed blade. She mastered it on several of the corpses they had shot in back alleys and once in the back of a Chevy van. Ear to ear surgical slits were her specialty.

Billy met Carla's piercing glance as he sipped his whiskey and felt faint. An ice shaft drove down his spine as she smiled and brandished a little wave. Freddy and Max and the rest of his crew saw his face melt and looked in Carla's direction. None of them spoke for a full minute. Freddy finally broke the silence.

"Wassamatta, Billy boy, you look like you seen a spook or somethin."

"No spook, man. Take a look at those two broads over there. First of all, what are they doing in our bar? And who in hell is that tall one? Check out those damn green eyes, would you? And those legs go up to her neck. Jesus H. Christ I never saw nuthin' like that before. Cept Adriana Lima, maybe, but only in those Victoria's Secret ads and stuff."

Freddy stole a quick look and turned back to Billy's boys, his face paling by the second. "Holy shit. What the fuck is that? Did she just fall off a magazine cover? Is she even real?"

"I think I recognize her," said artist wannabe Carl MacArthur. "Mighta seen her in the papers. Yeah, that's it, she was in the news some years back. Arranged for one of her gang to get her pilot's license and drop a coupla huge World War Two era bombs on an entire city block in Charleston. I think they were distracting everybody in the area while they walked off with some pricey paintings from an art auction around the corner. Somethin' like that. Made a lot of dough, those of 'em that managed to stay outta jail."

Billy finished his shot, chased it with a fresh beer, this time a snootier Heineken and then asked Sam for another shot. He slugged it down, then stepped outside for a cigarette. None of the rest of them said much for the next ten minutes while he got his bearings and walked back into the bar. Little Freddy, the best looking of the bunch, looked Billy in the eyes. "You're lookin' a wee bit better, old timer. Now watch how the pros do it."

Freddy hitched up his grease stained jeans and smoothed his shirt, took a deep breath and walked over to meet Carla and Joanna. "Well hello, ladies. Name's Freddy O'Brien. Ain't seen you here before, you lovely girls new in the area?"

"Watch the 'girls' shit, you old fart," spat Joanna. "We're grown women. Professionals. Armed and dangerous. Got it?" Carla shot her a warning glance. They were all that alright, but no sense in advertising the weapons stash. She high beamed her disarming man killer green eyes at Freddie and tried a peace offering.

"Hi there, yes we are rather new in the neighborhood. Heard about this place from a few of the locals and thought we'd drop in, watch some of the Pats game and knock a few cold ones back. Okay with you? I'm Carla by the way, and this is Joanna. We're up from Charleston. What pray tell do they call you again, young man?"

"Name's Freddy, ma'am, like I said. Freddy O'Brien. Folks call me Freddy."

"Yeah, we get the Freddy part. What do you and your, ah, gentlemen friends over there do with yourselves when you're not in here? No offense, but you fellas remind me of some of the bad dudes we met in prison years back."

"Oh, were you on guard duty or maybe social workers or something?" He knew that was bullshit. Nobody in prison looked like that.

"Actually no, Joanna and I did hard time for manslaughter and robbery. So did the other ladies in our, uh, squad shall we say."

"Funny you should mention that. We were thinkin' we maybe recognized you from the papers a while back. Something about stealing some paintings from an auction. Carl over there has a pretty good memory and he got us all thinkin' about it. Was he right?"

"I'm afraid so, Mr. Freddy. But quite honestly, a few of your pals over there look like ex-cons. Am I right about that?"

Freddy had never been hypnotized until this moment. His brain short circuited into its default mode, honesty. "You mind if I bring over the boss and introduce you? He's the guy with the goatee and Red Sox hat."

"Sure," Carla answered. Bring him over to say hello. But just him, okay? And don't try any funny stuff."

"You got it, be right back." Freddy headed back over to the bar and felt his knees tighten. Where was he going with this? He had no clue. Yet.

"Hey, Billy. Somebody wants to meet you."

"Yeah? And who might that be. Your fairy godmother?"

"Hey wise guy. I ain't no fairy, you big bozo. It's the big time looker over in the booth, the one you nearly passed out over. With her cute little friend there, the one with the paint splatters on her jeans. C'mon with me, just you. The rest of these guys can do, shall we say, quiet surveillance. Make sure we don't get mugged or nuthin'."

Billy nodded with all the calm and solemnity he could muster. He swallowed hard, took another shot, and tasted more fear in his throat than whiskey. He stepped in front of Freddy and they headed over to Carla's booth.

"Well good afternoon, ladies. I'm Billy O'Connell. This here's my friend Freddy. Guess you met already. I believe you're, uh, new here. Welcome to our little clubhouse. Are you enjoying the football game?"

Joanna had a wiseass retort ready but held her tongue. Carla was the boss. Always, absolutely always in charge.

"Yes we are, thank you for asking and introducing yourself. I'm Carla D'Andrea. An attorney out of Charleston. And my friend here is Joanna Ciampa. She's a very talented painter. Mostly works in Boston."

"What, like house painting or do you do cars and such?" The words had barely left his mouth when Billy felt like an idiot, his tongue beginning to Gorilla Glue to the roof of his mouth.

"No, actually. I'm an artist. Paintings and murals primarily, but I also do redesign work. Lobbies mostly, total modernizations and upgrades. I have a welder's license which comes in handy on some of the major projects."

Carla took an undetectable deep breath and leaned back in her seat. Flashed them those green eyes like neon lights on the Vegas strip. "Would you two fellows care to join us in a drink here? We like football but don't always know what just happened. Maybe you could help us with some of the play by play. Just go easy on the off color commentary. Ha, just kidding."

"Sure," Billy said. I'll go grab our drinks and ask Sam to bring us over another round. First, though, I'm gonna just go outside for a quick smoke. Come join me if you like."

Carla never smoked and didn't much care for the chilly weather outside, chilly at least by Charleston standards. "Thanks but I'll pass. Maybe Joanna would like to go with."

"Yeah, I'm game. Just grab one of my smokes and my purse maybe." She gently snagged her purse below the table and snaked a cigarillo from the pack without rustling her weapons.

Billy and Joanna stepped back out onto Billings Road and sat on the bench outside Danny's Hardware. They lit their smokes off Billy's Marine Corps Zippo and glanced up and down the street. A Quincy Police patrol car eased by, followed by a city bus and two young guys in an open convertible. Billy decided it was time to lean in.

"So, Joanna, what brings your friend Carla up to our fair city all the way from Charleston? Is it just the two of you or are there others in your circle?"

"Well, Carla's been here before and really likes the Boston area. And I'm a native here. I invited her and four of our cohorts here some years ago. It was sort of a retreat, you know, we needed some time to regroup. Get our act together. We camped out at the Four Seasons and had a couple meetings. To go with the clam chowder and all. Or is it chowdah?"

"Huh. Glad you all like it up here. Me and Freddy and the rest of our guys inside, we all grew up here. Went to Quincy High. Mostly started out okay after that but then…"

Joanna paused a long moment and fingered her cigarillo, finally taking a deep drag and blowing the smoke over her head. An Asian woman in her sixties came by with two toddlers in a stroller with a sack of groceries from the Chinese market up the street. After they passed she looked back at Billy.

"But then what? You guys fell off the wagon or something? Got in a little trouble? I don't mean to get too personal here, just curious. You know how it is with us girls."

Billy took two deep drags on his Camel filter and exhaled the blue cloud through his nose. How far should he go here? What kind of trouble could she possibly get him in at this point? Yeah, famous last words he thought.

"Let me just cut past the bullshit and tell you straight. You artists have good imaginations so let me hit the bottom line. Between us six pals, we were busted on a bunch of charges. Armed robbery mostly. But a coupla counts of manslaughter too. Don't worry, it was mostly only second degree. We've all done time in prison, sometimes two or three of us at once in the same cell block. Souza-Baranowski Correctional Center it was. Maximum security.

Pretty rough going in there but we all came out in one piece. Mostly, anyway. Max lost an ear and Mike a coupla fingers, but that don't slow 'im down too much. Me and Freddy mostly just lost our dignity. I'll never trust another brown guy again, or anyone plastered with tattoos. Buncha bullshit and you can keep every fuckin' nigger and gook in this life." The whiskey was doing the talking for him at this point and Billy knew it. He knew he sounded like a racist but what the fuck. But this lady was awfully nice to look at and she had some spunk, he decided.

Billy smoked another Camel while Joanna finished her cigarillo. He only had one pressing question for her at the moment. "You ladies ever do hard time?"

"Maybe we did, Billy. Maybe we did."

BAD SIGN

Billy and Joanna went back into the pub and joined Carla and Freddy in their booth. Carla was on her second margarita and no one had been keeping track of Freddy's drink count except their faithful bartender. Sam knew he was good for the cash tab as always. He was a regular. They all were. Well, except those two lookers over there.

"So, where were we?" Carla began. Joanna glanced at Billy and said "Comparing notes, basically. Seems like the four of us have some background in common. Commercial ventures of a sort. Adventures in commerce."

Carla threw back her head and laughed. "Yeah, that's one way of putting it. Freddy and I talked about that too. And the fact that in some ways, those were the good old days. Not the prices we paid, but the excitement. My shrink sometimes calls me an adrenaline junky. I get bored easily."

"Us too," Billy offered. "Nothing like the high you get from running a game on some bank or jewelry store. The money wasn't too bad either, right Freddy?"

"Yeah, man. Bought my kids some nice places in the Caribbean with some of the extra. And didn't you make some straight investments? Mutual funds or whatever they call 'em?"

"Mm," Billy mused. "Lots of mutual funds. They did pretty well over the years, too."

The Patriots game over, the Pats winning by a field goal, Sam had turned down the volume on the televisions and put on some music for them. First up was Cream's 2005 reunion concert at Royal Albert Hall in London. "Crossroads" and then "Born Under a Bad Sign" got them thinking about maybe getting their outlaw acts together. Carla wondered if she and her merry band might have some fun teaming up with Billy and Freddy's. She knew the men had several accomplices still sitting at the bar and wondered if maybe three from each side might, what was the right word, incorporate?

No, that wasn't it. Merge. Yeah, a temporary merger. That sounded better to her. The unmistakable baritone voice of Jack Bruce tracked her thoughts.

Born under a bad sign.
I've been down since I began to crawl.
If it wasn't for bad luck,
I wouldn't have no luck at all.
Bad luck and trouble's my only friend,
I've been down ever since I was ten.
Born under a bad sign.

Yeah, that's me, thought Carla. Big and *baaad.*

MARINA TIME

Carla asked Sam for a check for she and Joanna while Billy splurged for once and covered his gang of six. Two hundred bucks including a generous tip. Peanuts, if they could work something out with the ladies. If. What could possibly go wrong?

As they had agreed in the bar, eight of them met at Marina Bay in Quincy the next day. October 8, a glorious Saturday afternoon on Boston Harbor. Cotton puff ball clouds dotted the sky. Billy volunteered to give them his special walking tour of the area. They started at the huge parking lot off Victory Road. He wanted everyone to have a sobering image in the back of their minds to start their informal meeting. Some of the Quincy motorcycle cops were doing drills in the parking lot, which was dotted with orange cones. A police car was parked in the corner near a large puddle from the rain overnight. A half dozen **Harley-Davidson** FLHP Road kings weaved smoothly through the cones. Billy and Carla's entire group watched silently while the bikers trained.

The eight of them met servers Lizzie Lawless and Harriet Hunter as they strolled up the dock admiring the dozens of pleasure boats at their moorings. Oceans of pedestrians passed them by, most escorted by dogs of all breeds. Poodle mixes, all manner or terriers, labs, retrievers, some miniature somethings, French bulldogs, Maltese, a few basset hounds. All looked well taken care of, a few sporting colorful sweaters and vests. Carla didn't spot a guard dog in the bunch. She liked not seeing German shepherds or Dobermans. They would always remind her of prison and their ugly stinking handlers.

They turned around at Port 305 restaurant and headed back past the Marina Bay Living gift shop and dentist office, then Victory Point restaurant across from Marina Bay Market, and then up to the market itself. Several of the market's outdoor chairs were empty, so with the manager's permission they pulled them toward the benches abutting a small sandy lot. Carla decided it was time to formally introduce Billy and Freddy's gang to Lizzie and Harriet. As she began, another member of her team hopped out of a Yellow

Cab. Sally Harkin grabbed another chair and pulled it over. Freddie's first impression was that she acted like she owned the whole damned marina.

"Fellas, these lovely ladies here are my young friends Lizzie Lawless and Harriet Hunter. Yes, that's Lizzie's real name so you can dispense with the wisecracks. They both work behind the bars and as servers at several of the restaurants you see down here. Smile for us, ladies. And to their right, fresh out of her cab, is my gal pal Sally Harkin. Sally's a manager at Bank of America in Seaport. Right around the corner from where that big thee-A-tah was before the Covid done shut the mutha down. Oh mah, is that my southun accent creepin' through? Mah a-POL-o-gees."

At 34 Lizzie looked far too young to be an old hand with Carla but the men kept quiet about it. Her looks were distracting. Penetrating blue eyes, perfectly styled wavy auburn hair and an ocean blue midriff sweater and slacks right out of Riccardi's on Newbury Street in Boston. Great tits. A gold necklace with a pink sapphire pendant set off the outfit. Harriet appeared to be taking a day off from wiping spills and men off her tables. A simple black midriff top and pink shorts did the trick. The $400 Gucci aviator sunglasses were a nice accent against her ponytailed hair.

Harriet was a standard issue Irish redhead, ablaze with freckles dusting her pixie nose. She wore her hair in a bob or whatever they called it these days ad looked like she had fucked half of her customers for free, the other half for a few tokens of their affection. Like a trip to Barbados or a petite set of diamond studded gold earrings. Whatever it took, she was a business gal all the way.

She hadn't been raised that way. Catholic in fact. Mass every damn Sunday and brunch afterward. Her mother Katie was always strict, fair, paying attention to her young daughter. Father Mick was a distant prick to her. Successful at work due to his uncanny ability to turn on the charm at just the right moments. He even looked like a magician sometimes with his Don Ameche pencil mustache. His graceful swagger around the office punctuated the whole phony image. But he was still a prick at home, when he wasn't off playing golf with his bosses anyway.

Sally Harkin looked like a bank manager in Freddy's eyes. His line of work had caused him to meet dozens of them over the years. Forgettable grits and gravy face, medium height, shoulder length brown hair, dark eyes, not much discernable makeup and only a silver watch and small gold pinky ring for accessories. She had a plain Nordstrom purse under her left shoulder, her only concession to high end style or signal of wealth. Sally smiled all around and softly said, "pleased to meet y'all. And on such a pretty day."

Billy gazed overhead as a Sikorsky Blackhawk flew south from Boston. He wondered about the mission and how many crew it carried. Billy was friends with one of the locals at the marina who said he had worked at Sikorsky in Stratford, Connecticut a long time. Billy wondered what it was like to stand at the top of the stairway leading from the final assembly line up from a long metal staircase. To watch the worker bees in action. Then into the wire harness shop where nice middle aged white ladies painstakingly assembled the complex wiring systems that gave the company's products such amazing capabilities. Jack had told him it was something you never forgot, men and women at each station completing their exacting work and the necessary inspections before the aircraft itself or subassembly could move to the next station.

The next half hour was "chit chat city" in Billy's mind. He didn't complain out loud, especially since Carla's gang seemed happy enough with it. He felt a knot in the back of his neck and a shiver of adrenaline as the group laughed about exotic trips they fantasized about. Tahiti, Paris, Mozambique, South Africa. Nowhere he had ever been or thought much about.

Over and around the marina, birds enjoyed their days. Gulls swooped and soared, usually in pairs, sometimes in a damned squadron. Geese powered by, grebes flew in loose formations looking for productive fishing grounds. An occasional duck prowled the shallows poking at seaweed and muck.

The people watching kaleidoscope was always a kick. Pretty girls all over the place as usual but he was getting a little old for that. Well not really. The people who really stood out got his attention. A young man with dark hair, about five ten, whose face looked like a hatchet, wearing the obligatory week's worth of beard growth, reminded him of some guys he had done time with. Hatchet Boy finished his sandwich at one of the tables outside Marina Market before hurrying off. A short gal with a forgettable face, not talking, trailed after him. Were they related? Seeing each other? Who the hell knew. A fat woman pushing three hundred pounds in black leotards and powder blue top seemed oblivious to her mounds of overhanging flab. Thank God for the blond cutie pie with no bra and a pink tank top who came right behind chunk-o-meat. Then came two faggy looking guys with two fucking pit bulls. Yellow and purple streaked hair and god damned nose rings. Fucking *nose rings*. And the pussy behind them had another one. Holy shit, what's with all the pit bulls? Oh wait, maybe they're all rescues. Yeah, that had to be it. And he heard that not all of them were vicious. Depended on how they were raised.

A Katsiroubas truck delivering produce to the market drove by slowly. The driver, Ed Mullins, rolled his window down. "Hey Billy boy, how's it goin'?" "Just peachy, Eddy, can't complain. Even after the chemo!" Carla liked the fact that Billy seemed to know the neighborhood like the back of his weathered hands. Joanna wondered if he was a dealer in his spare time. Looking almost kindly and all, who would really suspect?

Carla changed places with Lizzie so she could sit next to Billy. She had a plan to bounce off the old man.

"So Billy, not to veer too far off the idle chatter, but I've been thinking about a gig we could do together. Me, Joanna and Lizzie, or maybe Sarah, you and Freddie to start. We'll keep the others in the background for a little while."

"Whacha got in mind? Shoot."

Carla thought about the firepower in her purse and then brushed off his implied reference to guns. "We can see that you guys are all doing fine outside of prison again. Successful even. So are we. Money is no problem, we all work and managed to squirrel away a lot of our take back in the day. But there's something missing now. Excitement. That adrenaline high you get from pulling off a big one. Know what I mean?"

Billy scratched at his goatee. "Yep, I do. Nothing like a big heist and clean getaway, that's for sure. Did you have a specific, uh, *project* in mind for us?"

"Matter of fact, yes. There's that big vault-like Bank of America at 1400 Hancock Street. Reminds me a little of Grand Central. The manager isn't the sharpest knife in the drawer and she's only got one teller working most lunch hours. Sometimes there may be nine or ten dazed customers in line, including some of those miniature old Asian ladies. No offense to gooks or anything, I'm just reporting details at the scene."

"You're not suggesting we do a holdup, are you? Silence. Yeah I think you are. What, and we come in fully armed but looking all innocent like regular customers? Sure, I get that. But talk to me, Carla. Tell me what you got."

CROSSROADS

Carla elaborated on a scheme for five of them, two from Billy's and three from hers. A week of detailed planning followed. They were locked and loaded. Back at Marina Bay for a final powwow before launching their attack on Bank of America, they sat and watched seagulls soaring overhead on a brisk breeze. A chubby Hispanic kid, about eighteen, shoved a cart containing four cases of beer up the ramp on his way to the Reel House restaurant. A few minutes later he came back down the ramp in front of them with four empty kegs, his orange t-shirt looking a little damper, and black pants. Nice dead end job, but honest anyway and folks did get parched in this neighborhood. They drank so much beer, in fact, that it was one of the best -selling items in the market and, lo and behold, a micro-brewery with four taps was opening up next door. Break Stone, the sign said.

Construction of the little brewery included plans for a game room, bathrooms of course, and plenty of seating. No food would be served, according to Kirk, the foreman of the construction crew. Lean as a whistle with a friendly smile and handshake for anyone with a question about their work, he constantly wandered in and out of the building, usually on his phone. Billy asked him if he ever did any "real work" or just let his men do everything. "I work from the neck up," grinned Kirk. "That's what I went to college for."

Carla liked Kirk. She loved that wide cowboy grin. He vaguely reminded her of Clint Eastwood in his much younger days. She always had a thing for Eastwood, wished she could meet him sometime. But this kid was right here and although she noticed his wedding ring, she wondered what it would be like to put on her cowgirl hat, sit on his face and ride him into a double orgasm. Just come all over him until he couldn't breathe and begged her to get off. Yeah, she thought, that's the ticket. Maybe then take a selfie of the two of them and send it to Eastwood with lots of hearts and flowers. She was pretty quick with emoji's too. Then she would help Kirk to his feet and offer to wipe him off. Like a nurse. Nurse Carla, with Joanna attending.

Keg Boy made everyone thirsty and they agreed to head up to Reel House, the nicely appointed restaurant with the giant glass chandelier and cushy booths. Or they could sit on the deck and watch the sailboats and grebes. Knock back a few beers over some half shells. A dozen assorted oysters arrived on chipped ice with cocktail sauce and lemon wedges. The oysters were just right, cold and briny. They tasted like the sea. They tasted like heaven. A dozen of the jewels disappeared before they had a chance to touch their beers. Carla and Joanna savored Sam Adams Porch Rockers, Billy and Freddy slugged Harpoon while they waited for more oysters. Two servers brought them two dozen Island Creeks on pizza sized trays. They vanished in eight minutes.

Two more rounds of beer and another eighteen oysters later, Billy, Freddy, Carla, Sarah and Joanna got down to business. They were immediately joined by Lizzie Lawless, who had been working at Chantey at the south end of the dock, behind Siros restaurant. Terrific clam chowder and fried calamari, generous drinks. Lizzie smiled that sparkly Lizzie smile that always wowed her customers and said "Hey gang, this looks like a party. So let's *pah-tay!*" For a server she was dressed to kill. Poured on black leather pants, navy t-shirt under a pink blouse. A tiny anchor tattoo adorned her left forearm. Pretty in pink, Carla mused.

Billy asked their server to bring them a bottle of Hennessy and five shot glasses. The bartender smiled and handed him a tray, even though he knew full well they weren't allowed to serve bottles of liquor. What the fuck, he figured. What's the worst they can do, fire my ass? As they began their toasts, Carla thought about the Cream revival concert playing in the background and the poignant lyrics to one of their standards, Crossroads. Eric Clapton carried the lead on vocals while Jack Bruce and Ginger Baker backed him on a detonating classic rock foundation.

I went down to the crossroads
Tried to flag a ride
Down to the crossroads

Tried to flag a ride
Nobody seemed to know me
Everybody passed me by
Going down to Rosedalez1

Yeah, that's it, Carla thought. We're at a crossroads alright. But we better not be sinking down. No after all we've been through. Not now.

WANDERLUST

Carla thought about that song and the incredible band, one for the ages, that produced this song. She let her mind wander to an era and a world far away. The great bands from the 1930s such as Glenn Miller and Artie Shaw were taking a break from their tour schedules. A booming voice that sounded a lot like Jack Bruce invited them to sit in an auditorium and listen to his band Cream, an invincible voice from 75 years in the future. Front row seats of course. The guys sat back and listened. Some could not wrap their brains around this style of music but most of the men sat enthralled. They knew they were gazing into a crystal ball, one that had their names inscribed on the base.

Carla felt a tingle at the back of her neck contemplating this gauzy image. Her adrenaline was kicking in. She could feel it like a tropical storm coming on. She was ready to rock 'n' roll with Billy's boys. Damn the fucking torpedoes.

The bottle of Hennessy half gone, the five of them had a plan. A mission. They would start with a major bank, just for practice. Bigger jobs would lie ahead.

Two days later it was Saturday, warm and fresh with a kicky breeze coming off the harbor. Dawn had poked its sleepy head up hours ago.

Carla wore a dark business suit, fedora and sunglasses. Her hypnotic green eyes downplayed if not hidden. Joanna wore a fresh army green jumpsuit with her blond hair back under a flowered blue bandanna. Lizzie had been instructed to look like Miss Anyone USA, as plain as possible given her stunning everything. Sarah was her regular self, at least she thought so at the time.

Billy and Freddie dressed like Joe and Tony Quincy. Blend right in. Clean jeans and golf shirts, boat shoes. Freshly shaved. Billy had swapped his new Rolex for an Invicta Pro Diver men's automatic 40mm stainless steel case with black dial. Model 8926 for those keeping score. He had ditched the jade pendant and gold wristbands. Couple of ordinary guys standing behind Carla and Joanna with Lizzie riding shotgun. Sarah Fiedler, Slingshot" herself, tried to just blend in, not that difficult given her naturally retiring nature. A teller waved Carla to the counter. She deposited $500 into her checking account and asked about securing a loan for a sailboat she had her eye on. Teller lady Shirley smiled and pointed her to the bank manager, Kendra Sutton. Carla met the manager and was ushered in to see their senior loan officer while Joanna advanced to the window.

Appearing outwardly fine when he entered the bank, Freddy gasped and grabbed his chest, fell to his right knee and feigned a heart attack. Sutton called 911 and asked for an ambulance. While Carla chatted up the loan lady, Joanna smiled at the teller and said she wanted to make a withdrawal.

"That's fine, just put your debit card into the machine and…"

"Actually, I don't have my debit card on me right now, so sorry, but I was hoping you'd take this." She snagged the Magnum Research Desert Eagle from her handbag, half draped under a handkerchief. "Your manager is assisting another customer so you're going to take me back into the vault and give me all the cash you can fit in my bag. You have five minutes. Got it?"

Teller Jenny Carson's face blanched and she began to stutter. "Let's go, sweetie, and throw a nice wave at the customers behind me, tell them you'll be right back." Billy and Freddie smiled politely and waved back. "No problem," Billy said. "We're on our lunch break.

Back in the vault, Jenny shook so hard she could barely manage the intricate locking system. She had only been back there a half dozen times in the past five years. Joanna kept the gun pointed at Jenny's head and told her to hurry up. Just to emphasize her haste, Joanna shot Jenny in her right foot as the vault swung open. "Oh, so sorry, I was aiming for your left elbow. This darned gun, don't know how our Navy Seals deal with it."

Jenny wailed in anguish before Joanna kicked her aside, pulled out her knife and punctured her larynx. "There, that should take your mind off your foot and keep the noise down, you know? Don't want those nice customers out there getting upset now, do we?"

Joanna filled her bag and a satchel she grabbed from inside it. She stuffed both of them with neat bundles of hundreds in three minutes and began to walk back toward the lobby. Miss Manager was escorting the paramedics in to tend to Freddy as Joanna strolled out the front door and hailed a cab. She got in with both bags and told the driver she was headed to Harvard Square. The driver waited at the lights and then headed over to I-90.

Carla eventually sauntered out of the loan officer's office, telling her she would need to talk to her attorney about the terms and conditions. "So nice to have met you, Dorothy, thanks so much for your help."

She walked outside and met Lizzie, Billy, Sarah and Freddie. They walked down Hancock Street two blocks and called for an Uber. For everyone except Lizzie. The driver arrived in ten minutes. "Going up to Harvard Square folks?"

"Yes sir, thanks. Looks like it's still a nice day for a ride to Cambridge. And this sure beats the train, ya know?"

Once in Cambridge, the squad checked into the Sheraton Commander Hotel. They booked two suites so they could stretch out and keep the men separate. Carla put everything on her American Express card and asked Sarah to run out and get them some inauspicious changes of clothing. She returned in forty-five minutes carrying four bags. Carla ordered champagne for all of them and sat on the plush red velvet couch overlooking Garden Street. Lizzie looked out the window and saw no official vehicles. No ambulances or fire trucks, no squad cars. Not even a delivery truck. Three seagulls flew by squawking per environmental and Audubon regulations.

A hotel kid from the kitchen knocked at the door with an enormous cart. He came in and unloaded two bottles of Perrier-Jouët Belle Epoque champagne, two buckets of ice, two silver cups of Beluga caviar, a six pack of Harpoon, a bag of Doritos and some mixed nuts. Joanna gave him two hundred dollar bills for a tip. He looked at her with a blank expression so she gave him another three Benjamins. This time he stuttered something incomprehensible and tripped over the cart on his way out. Carla thought she decoded a "g-g-gee th-thanks" and roared with laughter. Tears came to her emerald green electric eyes and within seconds they were all laughing until they started seeing stars.

The kid finally gone back out, Freddy popped the champagne and poured himself a glass and then more for Carla, Sarah and Joanna. Billy helped himself to the beer and Freddy lit a cigarette. Carla bellowed "Open up all the damn windows, kiddo!" Lighting a cigarillo, Joanna pitched in with a snort. "Wanna get something done, call in a woman you wienie!"

Joanna sat back down on the couch next to Carla and dumped out the money. They all grabbed stacks of bills and began thumbing through the money. Five minutes later Carla asked for counts. She went first. "$70,000 even." Then Joanna: "$65k." Then Billy: "another 40." Sarah had forty. Freddy had seventy. "So that makes 285 grand. Not bad for a start, eh?" Another roar of laughter and a second round of drinks. Joanna said "Here's to Stuttering Steve with the cart! Maybe I should ask the little twerp out later!"

Carla couldn't resist. "Joanna, you ignorant slut. Ask him to finish speech therapy first so you don't need a fucking translator. Then ask him how big his Johnson is and see if he can talk straight. Just a little test."

Sarah had wandered over to the living room window and peered out at the gulls and a single hawk gliding by. A Boston police car pulled up to the curb followed by one statie. A soggy blanket of motion sickness fell on the suite. Freddy was visibly nauseous, like he had just ingested a bowl of warm tarter sauce. Carla, Joanna, Billy and Freddy pulled out their guns. They all attached silencers.

Officers Wingo, Ruskin, Wiggins and O'Hara ranged from six feet to six three. All veterans of their respective forces, all fit and strong as stallions. Charles Wingo and Bill Ruskin led the pack, right hands near their holsters. They rode the elevator up in near silence. Wingo whispered "Sometimes this job sucks, but not today amigos. Today feels special somehow." Rusty Wiggins and Doug O'Hara banged on the door to the suite. "Police, open up."

Carla walked toward the door and opened it, her Glock in her right hand, hidden. "Well hello, officers, to what do we owe the pleasure?

"Are you Carla D'Andrea?" Wiggins asked, flashing his badge.

"Yes, that's me."

"We need to come in for a minute, ma'am. We have some questions for you and your, ah, friends."

"Sure, come on in. We were just enjoying a drink. Can we get you some water?"

Wiggins strode in first without answering her. As the rest of his team rolled through the door, Carla, Joanna, Billy and vomit stricken Freddy let loose. All four officers were blasted in the chest, two shots each. They crumpled to the floor in a torrent of copper smelling blood, Wiggins and O'Hara on top of each other. They barely made a sound as they twitched in agony, Ruskin's hand grasping for his radio.

Carla and Billy dragged all four officers into the living room before shooting each of them in the right ear and through their carotid arteries. Joanna guessed at least six liters of blood quickly soaked the carpet as all motion on the floor stopped. The air stank of pennies, champagne, beer and almonds. Mostly copper, Freddy figured as he puked over the couch into the edge of the blood. He wiped his face with a blue and white linen napkin, then gargled some champagne and spit it on O'Hara. Then puked again, this time violently on himself.

Carla surveyed the mayhem and took charge. "OK, guys, we're out of here. Right fucking now. Billy, get us an Uber van. But make sure whatever you get is here right away. Everybody grab anything they have that could identify any of us. We'll leave our bags here and the, ah, fucking mess for housekeeping and the detectives, ME's, morgue guys and the rest. Y'all know the drill. Now move it!"

They were down on the street in five minutes. The car Billy ordered was just pulling to the curb. He checked the license for a match to the number on his phone and the driver. LHX984, Delgado. Bingo. They eased into the red GMC Savana and headed to Quincy, slick as duck grease. By prior arrangement, they kept the conversation light and chatty. The ride down I-90 was bumpy as usual but uneventful. The sun was well on its way down and darkness began its descent. As they turned down Seaport Drive and passed Atria Assisted Living, they saw a big ass coyote walking against traffic along the grass bordering the woods. Carla smiled and saluted him. "Buena caza, mi amigo. Mucho buena caza."

Their Uber driver Delgado, a wiry 40 year old man from Columbia and father of three teenage sons, made a right at the end of Seaport Drive onto Victory Road and headed toward a huge white faced condo building with a blue light on every porch. He eased to a stop and Carla's gang strode onto the sidewalk, tossing thankyou's and have a nice day's at Delgado. Joanna slipped him a huge tip for a half hour ride, a crisp Benjamin. He nodded and smiled back graciously before heading off to his next pickup in South Boston. Carla and Billy led the way up to the sixth floor and they all settled in to the two bedroom unit. Joanna, the artiste herself, had decorated everything to a tee, complete with several of her own paintings, lush furniture, and French provincial lamps. The purple carpeting was clean enough to dine off. The fridge was stocked with steaks, red potatoes, salad fixings, beer and champagne. A bag of el primo Columbian weed rested in the silverware drawer. Sarah went out on the balcony and lit the grill. The atmosphere was lovely, 72 degrees with a light breeze, the stars dusted over Boston Harbor. Dozens of boats swayed at their moorings like sailors just getting their land legs back under them.

HOME ON THE RANGE

Carla, Billy and their gang swept out to the porch and nestled into the matching lounge chairs that Joanna had ordered for them. Freddy hustled them all some chilled champagne glasses and a bottle of Laurent-Perrier Brut Millesime 2008 in a silver chalice overflowing with chipped ice. He surprised everyone by pulling an envelope of cocaine out of his shirt pocket. Around the porch it went on a hand held mirror. Only Sarah declined. Carla offered a toast.

"Here's to some pretty smooth operators. We had to send a few cops up into the clouds today, but they did come looking for trouble. We hadn't done anything wrong in Cambridge in quite a while. Anyway, job well done ladies and gentlemen. A toast to your health!"

Five glasses of champagne disappeared under the starlight in moments. Another bottle of Laurent Perrier appeared in their bucket as if by magic, courtesy of Sarah. She hustled inside to toss out the first bottle before settling back into her seat outside. Their poor fragile Sarah had initially chosen to not join them on the Cambridge jaunt, preferring to wait for them in the Quincy condo. Glowing ember smiles lit everyone's faces like a campfire in the desert.

Their building faced another massive condo structure designed by the same unimaginative architect. Carla spotted a small gathering on the opposite porch, a successful looking man in late middle age, full head of close cropped grey hair, who was still wearing wraparound sunglasses when the stars bubbled out. A bottle blonde, slightly younger, sat beside him drinking white wine. To their left, in the corner, sat a thin young man with prep school-short sandstone hair. Carla noted that the couple, probably his parents, picked at a snack tray while the boy remained silent. After a few minutes, four others joined them on the porch. Two more bottle blondes still in their twenties and a handsome young hunk of a dark haired man with an obligatory week old growth of beard in a blue t-shirt. The adults sat elbow to elbow, chatting up a storm while the kid looked on passively. Carla's brain stirred from the champagne as she sized up an opportunity.

Midnight at the oasis. Carla's head swam from a busy day avoiding apprehension with her team. One by one the others had drifted off. Joanna had managed to find a bed to collapse in. Sarah was close behind her. Neither one of them made it into their nightgowns and lay like ragdolls who somehow made it through the spin cycle but not into the dryer. Billy and Freddy snored like lumberjacks on the porch. The champagne long gone, they had snaked the last two beers out of the refrigerator before weaving their way back out. Each of the Heinekens remained clutched in their paws, flat and lifeless as the sun's first light brought on the new day.

The mayhem they had committed yesterday was now a dimming memory. Two aging black women from housekeeping discovered the ghastly mess in Cambridge not long after the massacre. They stumbled screaming down the hall, rode the elevator down to the lobby and assailed Bart at the desk.

"Oh Mr. Bart, Mr. Bart," shrieked Edith, sucking in air like a dying Covid-19 patient. "There's a frightful mess up there in 1400."

"Oh come on, ladies, it can't be that bad. Would you like me to send a maintenance guy up there with one of our heavy duty vacuum cleaners or something?"

"Oh no sir, Mister Bart, no sir," croaked Mary Elizabeth. You need to call the police. Homicide people need to get in there and people with body bags. Medical examiners or whatever like I seen on TV. Plus I've been reading this Harlan Coben fellow, and Dennis Lehane. The crime thriller novelists. Professionals like they're always talking about."

The color in Bart's face drained into a puddle on the desk. His tongue felt plastered to the roof of his mouth. "Hello 911, yes, this is Bart at the Sheraton Commander Hotel in Cambridge. I think we've had a multiple homicide here… how many bodies ladies? Yeah, four dead men. Cops and state troopers. I just came on duty so I didn't see them come in but their cars are still outside. Yes, right away, please. Ten minutes? Okay great, I'll be here with our staff members who found the officers. Thank you, ma'am."

Carla, Billy and their entourage slept until 10:30 before a squadron of noisy seagulls cresting on the easy breeze slowly roused them from the depths. They mustered everyone out on the porch and quietly gave out assignments. Blue eyed and demure Sarah, still lithe and lovely at 45, drew weapons cleaning and reassembly. Joanna cleaned up the mess they had made eating and drinking. She had to drag out a mop to get rid of all the dip that had splattered the decking and some spot remover to clean the furniture. Carla groped through the closets looking for suitably cool and coordinated outfits for the ladies to wear to brunch.

At 11:15 they moseyed down to Victory Point restaurant. Ordering for the table, Carla asked their server Alexis for eggs benedict, seafood over pasta, fried calamari, chopped salad and clam chowder. This was preceded by vodka tonics and shots of Grey Goose. They asked for three pots of strong coffee after regaining their bearings with a major assist from the flock of liquid geese.

Boston harbor and the dock at Marina Bay simmered with activity. Half a dozen boat owners and fisherman rigged for striped bass trolling. A 25 year old bronzed blonde girl in a miniscule bikini, sailor hat and deck shoes got everyone's attention, as did her strapping boyfriend. To their surprise, the girl took the wheel as Prince Perfect tossed a cooler on board and cast off.

Their little craft was the Prawn Princess. Carla noted what an odd name that was, given that there wasn't a shrimp swimming within 500 miles of the dock. But it reminded her to order shrimp cocktail and raw oysters for all of them.

Madam String Bean continued to preside over their little gathering on the dock. She quietly went around the table, smiling and asking questions.

Everyone affirmed that they had finished their assignments without offering details. She let them know that there would be follow-up work to be doled out once they got back upstairs to the condo.

They took an hour and a half to devour all the food and coffee. All the while chatting up every passerby who was accompanied by a dog. They decided that the cutest one of the bunch by far was a Lhatese puppy named Jodi. An elderly man wearing a navy cap and wielding a red cane was obviously her owner. He stopped to make small talk while Jodi went around the table in a blur of white fluff. Joanna noted that she reminded her of a little white fur ball hurricane. The owner said that he got that all the time from people. Also how darn cute she was, but how it never got old. He and his son had found her at a pet store nearby, or rather she found them. "Take me! Take me!" she pleaded while pounding on the Plexiglas enclosure. Naturally they did. They absolutely had to. Docile on the ride home, she exploded once she had a look around. "I'm home! I'm home! Yahoo! Let's rock 'n roll!"

DUMBASS AMERICANS

The sun warmed them like a long lost friend. They began to get full of the "great eats" as Freddy put it. And just a little of themselves. Carla launched them into a discussion on human stupidity, a plague that only seemed to be getting worse in America. *Stupid*, Carla offered as a baseline from Merriam-Webster, meant pretty much what most people thought, those that actually could think, that is. *Slow of mind; obtuse; given to unintelligent decisions or acts; acting in an unintelligent or careless manner; marked by unreasoned thinking or acting. Senseless.*

She laid it all out for them in black and white. They all knew stupid people, and in fact depended on them when it came to picking victims and unwitting accomplices. Fortunately, these turds were ubiquitous. Oddly enough, almost everyone (93%) thinks they are an "above average" driver. Worse, some *90%* of Americans believe that they have an above average ability to discern the truth regarding the myriad "news" blurbs that they run across. Most people think they're more attractive than others do. Gosh they're *GREAT!* And for decades, men thought they were flat out smarter than women, as countless idiotically sexist ads flouted men's superiority in everything except cooking (sometimes), washing dishes and laundry. And people bought it. Spent their money on it. Yikes.

Scientific American had put it this way: *"Inflated perceptions of one's physical appearance is a manifestation of a general phenomenon psychologists call "self-enhancement."* Researchers have shown that *"people overestimate the likelihood that they would engage in a desirable behavior, but are remarkably accurate when predicting the behavior of a stranger. For example, people overestimate the amount of money they would donate to charity while accurately predicting others' donations."*

Carla had several psychologists as former legal clients in Charleston who preferred to call most of this self-aggrandizement sheer ego defensive stupidity. No, pal, you're not a really generous, nice looking political savant and a pro behind the wheel. You're a schmuck.

Even a casual glance at IQ data in this country revealed a disturbing downward trend in recent years. John R. Schindler wrote in the Observer that *"If you're imagining that the population around you is getting dumber, you're right. This has become a legitimate crisis for the U.S. military, which is having a devil of a time finding sufficient numbers of recruits who are not stupid, obese, and/or convicted criminals."* The U.S. military, especially today, demands that recruits are of course bright enough to understand and operate complex weapon systems and equipment, tactical decisions and their role in carrying them out.

Per the Pentagon's data, a whopping 71 percent of young Americans are ineligible to join the armed forces once they disqualify those among the 34 million Americans ages 17-24 who are too stupid, obese, and/or have criminal records. Holy shit. *Seventy-one per cent.* Imagine if we had to win World War II after tossing aside nearly three quarters of candidates in the service pool. Think operating and maintaining Navy warships, crawling through the jungles of Bataan and other Pacific islands, or battling hostile forces in Europe while freezing was simple? Uh, no. And we will forevermore commemorate Memorial Day because of the not only brave but *thinking* Americans who gave their lives to a just cause. On a destroyer, in a tank or the trenches, on a bomber or in a fighter plane. Take your pick.

Carla was on a roll. Couple more examples she felt compelled to point out. Forty per cent of Americans believe that in their present form, humans have existed for about 10,000 years. The true answer is closer to 200,000. Two thirds of Republicans believe that Trump was the legitimate winner of the 2020 presidential election 2020… despite zero evidence or court proven claims of sufficient fraud *anywhere* to have tipped the outcome to Biden. And let's not forget the over 30,000 false statements or outright lies perpetuated by Trump while he held office. Or right wing media's insistence that the January 6 insurrection was driven by left wing extremists or the FBI.

Theproblem, Carla explained, is that millions of Americans get their "news" from screwy, biased, inaccurate sources. Fox News, a popular source of information among older whites, rates lower than average in most evaluations by independent experts. She pointed out that Fox no longer says "fair and balanced."

"Wow, y'all" Carla wondered sarcastically, those man killer green eyes fluttering at a passing moron and two gargantuan slobs who looked pretty Fox-y to her, "Which one of those fucking losers looked in the mirror before they went out today?"

Billy put his sixth beer down and looked around the table. This seemed as good a time as any to pontificate a little himself and lay down some thoughtful (he thought) suggestions.

"First, and obviously my friends, we need to look at our educational system, a massive topic in itself. While Americans can brag about having the best colleges and universities in the world, K-12 is a whole different story. By the way, most folks think pretty highly of their own kids' school system. A lot higher than they rate other schools. My challenge to everybody is this: are we teaching our kids skills that will help them separate facts, science and technical expertise from, ah, bullshit? It's scary how many folks get their news from Facebook, for example, among other social media sites that're basically just trash. I've got nothing against social media per se, but how many of our kids and young folks are consistently encouraged to scour relatively reliable news sources? Like Reuters. Or the New York Times, Washington Post, NPR, BBC, CNN, Time Magazine? Huh? Even the Huffington thing is far superior to fucking Fox. How many teachers take the time to assign news for the kids to read so they can be discussed objectively in class? It sure never happened in my day at a pretty solid public high school."

Carla picked the ball back up and chimed in. "Yeah, Billy, you're right. As for parents. Probably most of them could do a much better job of helping their kids navigate their way through the tsunami of easy access and often unreliable, inaccurate news sources. Hey, Johnny, how about putting that dumbass Facebook, TikTok and Instagram aside for a while and talk with your dad and me about this article on Bloomberg? Or this one in Forbes? They've got some good stuff to say about what kinds of great jobs are out there for you. And some really cool ideas. Or, 'How 'bout we hit the science museum this weekend? We could grab an early dinner at Appleby's or someplace afterward. C'mon, whaddya say?'"

Joanna had been itching to chime in. "OK now for high school curricula. My high school offered psychology basics during the summer but most schools don't touch it and most kids' first exposure to psychology coursework doesn't come until college. Maybe we could encourage more kids to look more objectively at how we social animals usually process data and our own experiences in a way that protects our egos rather than elevates truth. Yeah, we all need a few defenses but we tend to overdo them at the expense of confronting the world and ourselves truthfully. Hey, remember that line from ET, this is *reality*, Greg?"

Back to Billy, one of the pontificators in chief for a day. "Schools also do a crappy job teaching history. A 2014 report I read by The National Assessment of Educational Progress showed that only eighteen percent … eighteen fucking percent… of American high school students were proficient, I think that was the word they used, in US history. The problem runs pretty deep. A 2012 or maybe 2013 story in Perspectives on History magazine found that eighty eight percent of elementary school teachers considered teaching history a low priority. But as this fellow David Cutler said in The Atlantic magazine, and I quote, high school history doesn't have to be boring. By tying past events to contemporary issues, teachers can move beyond rote memorization end quote. Sure wish someone had told my teachers that."

A distinguished looking guy in his late sixties or so at the next table had been listening in. "Hey you guys, my name's Arthur, and excuse me for sort of eavesdropping your conversation and butting in like this, but you all sound like pretty smart cookies. If I may divert your conversation just slightly, and seeing that I have, uh, a few years on most of you… I've been thinking about some pretty heady stuff myself."

"Go on, Arthur" answered Carla. "We're listening you old fu… timer."

"Yeah ok, thanks. Old timer, you got that right. I'm eighty six by the way. And I'm entering into this new season of my life, unprepared for all the aches and pains and loss of strength and the ability to go and do things that I never did but wish I could now. Every day now, getting a shower is a real target. And taking a nap isn't a treat anymore, it's mandatory."

"Cause if you don't on your own you just fall asleep where you're sitting," prompted Joanna.

"Yes ma'am, and I have regrets, there are things I wish I hadn't done. And things I should have done but somehow didn't. But you know what? There are lots of things I'm happy to have done and it's all in a lifetime. So if you're not in your winter yet let me remind you, it will be here quicker than you think. So whatever you would like to accomplish in life, do it quickly. Life is a gift to you. And a gift to those who come after. Live it like you goddamn mean it. And forget those stupid stinking bucket lists. Just do what you enjoy and try making other people happy for as long as you can. There. End of speech."

Arthur's Hallmark card-y soliloquy finally over, Carla and her gal pals split the check with Billy's boys and then headed back to the condo to sleep off the heavy lunch and drink. They were fast asleep when Carla's cell phone rang.

SPOT CHECK

"Hello? Who's this?"

"It's Bart from the Sheraton Commander Hotel in Cambridge. You may recall staying with us before leaving so abruptly. And without paying, either, for which I could have you arrested. When the cleaning crew got to your room they found quite the, um, disaster scene. Four dead officers from the local police and Massachusetts State Police mangled in a sticky pool of blood. Each one of them, according to the medical examiner who was here, had been shot four times. What can you tell me about this?"

Carla knew better than to stay on the line with him since he could quickly track her location. "How horrible, how could that have happened? I know nothing about it," she said before hanging up. She immediately woke up Joanna and Sarah and reported the conversation to them.

"Holy fucking shit," said Joanna. "I'd say you were kidding us but I know you better than that. I guess we had better get out of here immediately before that smartass sends the cops after us. If he hasn't already, that is."

Sarah was too scared to speak. Instead, she brushed her teeth and hair, packed a bag, called Yellow Cab and asked for her friend Ronnie to pick them up.

They had hoped that this would not be necessary, but Carla insisted that they plan for the worst. As she always did. Like a well rehearsed 1930's big band, maybe Glenn Miller or Artie Shaw, they bolted into action. Pack only bare essentials. Toiletries, jewelry, cash, two days' worth of clothes, plus every weapon they had. Make the place look like they'd be right back. Put out a vase of fresh flowers in the living room picked from the porch.

All in ten minutes, just in time to pile into Ronnie's cab and head for comparatively grimy Dorchester, a half hour and a quarter world away. Destination Little Manor, a colonial looking mini-mansion set on a pool table smooth green lawn surrounded by pines. Carla did that runway model stroll of hers up to the desk and poured on the southern belle charm with her former model friend Charlotte.

Little Manor was a misleading name for a hotel, just the way owner Robby Robbins liked it. Dorchester had pretty much always been a solid place to grow up, with stately churches, decent if not stellar schools, plenty of restaurants and taverns. Pretty much a working class city, solid as a rock. Little Manor stood out because it almost looked like it was kidnapped from back Greenwich, Connecticut. Almost. Walking in the front entrance felt like stepping back in time to a more stable, predictable elegance. Although you found the place by searching for hotels, it was actually a bed and breakfast.

The rooms were elegantly decorated and the breakfasts alone were almost worth booking a stay. Everything about the place, including the Olympic sized pool, was spotless. If you wanted to get away from the riffraff and anyone who didn't have a Caucasian pedigree, you felt comfortable. Like you were wearing a London tailored suit or a cashmere sweater. To go with the smug grin on your face.

Carla, Joanna and Sarah glanced around the lobby and smiled at each other. Carla approached Charlotte for a long overdue hug. They sensed and identified each other's perfume on lady autopilot. From Sephora.

"Hey Charlotte my girl, it's been way too long" Carla began. "Yes indeed," followed Charlotte, "and you certainly are a sight for these sore old eyes. Where on earth have you been the last few years and what have you been up to? And do by all means introduce me to your lovely friends."

"This is Joanna, my wing woman if you will, we go way back. She's from Boston originally and made her bones as probably the best freelance artist within 500 miles." Joanna was about to say 1,000 miles but she just beamed instead and almost sprouted freckles befitting a Girl Scout.

"And this is Sarah, we sometimes call her Slingshot. She was having a tough time in Charleston when I was working down there as an attorney. She came up to me while I was having a nice quiet... quiet, right Sarah?... glass of wine in a bar clutching her last seven dollars on earth, hoping to make a friend. That fair, Sarah?"

"Yup. Things were tough back then but I've come a long way thanks to these gals. I have never forgotten their kindness to a total stranger."

Charlotte helped them settle into their suite and asked if they had brought something to sun by the pool in. In the time it took them to think up an excuse for traveling so light, she returned with three bikinis and mauve robes. Problem solved. The guys could fend for themselves for now. That was Charlotte.

GAME ON

Once poolside, Joanna lit a cigarillo, stretched out on a chaise, and suggested they try their hands at playing what she called fun facts. She didn't really know where Billy and Freddy had gone but for the moment didn't care. They'd be fine, she assured herself. To her obvious delight, Carla and Sarah were all in, so she led off.

"Okay, you guys especially are gonna love this one. About 200 years ago, William Burke along with his friend William Hare figured that the medical school at Edinburgh University would pay for cadavers. Yeah, dead bodies. So these guys cooked up a plan to make money.

Hare was a landlord. He would rent to the poor in Edinburgh. Then Burkey boy would get a tenant loaded, wait for him to conk out, and then suffocate the fucker by sitting on his chest and smothering him. This sinister-- ha -- method eventually came to be called *burking*. Said stiff usually didn't show wouldn't have wounds or marks or anything. Naturally this made it much easier to sell the corpse.

Officially, ole Burkey and Hare bumped off sixteen people, but the actual body count was for sure higher. Eventually these guys were apprehended. Hare got immunity to testify against his pal Burke, who got his ass found guilty and hung. Ha! Burke's body, and here's some gen-u-ine irony, got donated to science. There was even a rumor that—get this, y'all-- the anatomy students who dissected his ass hung onto his body parts. Jesus H. Christ, they even used his skin to bind their books.

Not bad, eh? But getta loada this one. Although this story was never confirmed as fact officially…it's been around for a long time and never been disproved either. Ready? A few members of Al Capone's family, back in the 30's, got to puking after they drank some expired milk. So the all-time famous gangster pushed his weight around and started this campaign to get the first expiration dates on milk bottles. This is like back in the day when milk was delivered by horse drawn buggies. My grandma Bitty used to tell me about that, and how they'd keep the milk in ice boxes. So it looks like probably Capone did at least one good thing before they jailed his butt for tax evasion. That, ladies, is why every container of milk people buy today has an expiration date."

"Good one, Jo. My turn I guess" said Carla. You all know I like birds, right? OK, well the wedge-tailed eagle **is the biggest bird of prey** in Australia. The females are larger than the males and can weigh almost 12 pounds with a seven and a half foot wingspan. That's like longer than the biggest dude in the NBA. So on their own, they mostly nail rabbits and other little critters, in packs or whatever they call 'em, but they've been seen taking down grown ass kangaroos. These particular eagles really like to guard their turf, and have been seen attacking—get this-- small planes and freaking *helicopters* that get too close to their nesting sites."

Before she could applaud that one, Sarah noticed a car creeping up the driveway, a red 2012 Audi 100 CS. She thought she heard Pavarotti singing from the speakers. Fifty feet from the pool where they lounged, the car came to a stop and the driver slowly got out. Sarah thought he looked familiar and was about to call out when Joanna said, "hey Freddy, what are you doing driving back here? Did you come to ogle these gorgeous poolside bodies?" Freddy chuckled and that got them all laughing wildly, the kind of laugh that made their breasts jiggle in their skimpy swimwear.

"Well, ladies, I just figured I would kinda stop in again and check to see how you're doing. I've got the nice wheels from my cousin today and if you need anything let me know and I'll run out and get it."

Carla jumped on that opening like a cat on a stray mouse. "Come a little closer, Freddy, all of a sudden I feel like whispering. You know, it's so peaceful here, why make a racket?" Freddy ambled up to her and leaned over. "Sup girl?"

"Well, to be honest, we could probably use a little bit more, ah, security. Any chance you could find us an RPG launcher and some ammo? Like by tonight?" Freddy seemed locked and loaded, given his rapid fire response. "Sure, what kind you got in mind?"

"How about a -26 Aglen, can you do that?"

No ordinary weapon of war, the Russian made grenade launcher was designed to kill, maim and obliterate. Its single stage rocket with jackknife fins carries an explosive warhead that can bust through 440 mm of armor, a full meter of reinforced concrete or even a meter and a half of brick structure. With a maximum effective range of 250 meters and a loaded weight of just under six and half pounds, it could neutralize virtually any threat that Carla, Joanna and Sarah might face. Death on wheels, and hold the wheels. Freddy drove off with a wave in the rear view mirror. That Freddy. A true piece of work.

Joanna had another fun fact for her pals.

"Ok, y'all, you may know that coconut crabs are thieves. Matter of fact, they're so famous for this that they're also known as robber crabs. If something stinks enough or it's just shiny and they can get to it, them crabs will just lift it. I'm gonna try to quote from an article here. This research chick reported **an expensive thermal camera stolen that she had left out overnight to film Christma**s Island wildlife, and she knew humans weren't the culprit. And get this. At a family barbeque, 52 god damn coconut crabs **showe**d up uninvited and went right after the food."

"I don't think I can top that one," chuckled Carla. "Kudos, girl!"

Rocket Time

Carla and the gang decided to revisit the Irish pub in Quincy. They arrived in full cover girl regalia and joined the dozen old white guys seated at the bar watching women's tennis. A scrawny dude in his twenties sat at the bar in a white sleeveless T-shirt and black shorts drinking beer. He looked from side to side and occasionally chatted with the bartender, Paula, as she mixed drinks, poured draft beers and took cash for payment as one by one the old guys finished.

They were watching women's tennis on TV. The winner of one qualifying round was a brown haired girl with her mane pulled back in a tight don't-fuck-with-me sweep. She was in drop dead amazing shape. Her muscles loosened and flexed under a sheen of sweat. She was lean, mean, and ready for the kill. Carla could not resist commenting.

"Jesus fucking Christ would you look at that body. I could eat her up from head to toe and yes that includes her pussy in case y'all were wondering. Just lick those gorgeous lips and suck on her clit. Maybe wash it down with some champagne before she goes down on me. Clit for tat, ya know what I mean?"

Joanna looked at her with wide open blue ocean eyes and a gentle smile. "I'm going first if you don't mind. You can have sloppy seconds, my good friend. Better yet, you could do me while I'm doing her."

"Alright you queers, let's head back to the ranch. Freddy's probably waiting for us."

Freddy was back at the Dorchester bed and breakfast in two hours flat with the weapon from hell in a plain cardboard box that he had tied a handle to. It was heavy lifting and kicked his brain in gear. He smiled and said hello to Charlotte at the desk, and proceeded up to the ladies' suite. He tapped gently on the door before putting his ear to it to make sure they were around. The muffled sound he heard caused a bulge in his jeans. He patted it down and knocked harder. Carla came to the door wearing a bathrobe and slippers.

"Hey there Freddy boy, is that for us? Oh great and how the hell did you pull that off anyway?" Freddy looked like he had just swallowed a sweaty basketball sock. "Just had to see the right guys, that's all, piece a cake. Which pardon me but that looks like what you've been eating. By the way you owe me ten grand for this little baby. You can pay me next week if you don't have the cash handy, that would be fine."

Joanna came out of the bedroom smelling like girl next door heaven. She grinned at Freddy and said hey before peeking out the window. An unmarked squad car was creeping up the driveway. As it got closer, she recognized the two Dorchester cops. Alan McMaster and Dave Beck. She knew instantly what they were after. She tore open Freddy's box and yanked out the RPG, loaded it and went back to the window. She made sure to keep the curtain nearly closed and took aim at them.

The deafening blast and kick bounced her onto the couch. She cracked her head on the coffee table and could barely get up. Carla went to the window and said "holy fucking shit. So that's what these things can do. I don't even see those two fuckers, just a big red splat on the driveway and a smoldering pile of doors and tires. Well you guys, take a look at this. I think we really did it this time. Maybe a tiny bit of overkill, ya know? I'll have to think about that while we get our asses out of here. Sarah, pack everybody up into one bag while I go talk to my Charlotte downstairs. Joanna, can you hear me? OK good, get us that cabdriver friend of ours. Tell him to get here immediately and keep his damn mouth shut. Got that? I said you GOT THAT?"

DOWNTOWN

The Four Seasons hotel on Boylston Street in Boston's Back Bay was beyond elegant, dripping with forever dreams and snob appeal. The hotel boasted a well-deserved five star rating and its proximity to the Public Garden and Beacon Hill. Amenities stretched to the skies, including an indoor pool with a view, fancy bath products, a top rated restaurant, in-room goodies such as cribs, night lights and playpens. And, of course, over a dozen darned swell function rooms.

A husky back man greeted them at the door and held it open for them. Introducing himself as Ramone, he flashed a practiced smile that edged up an extra half inch when in the presence of such beautiful women. He had a lot of practice at that with the ritzy clientele they attracted.

Sally Anne Brinkley took their bags and brought them up to their suite. She nodded and executed a just slightly too cute southern courtesy when Carla handed her a hundred dollar bill. Their rooms featured views and beds like even they had seldom experienced. But it was all in a day's work for women who craved exciting new experiences like starving wolves.

As usual, they quickly found themselves getting hungry and looking for action. They took the elevator down to the second floor and walked into the very high end, a bit too full of itself Japanese restaurant, Zuma. They sat at the bar and within moments their server appeared out of thin air.

"Hello there, lovely ladies and welcome to Zuma," said Hiro. "What can I get for you this evening?" They all ordered tropical drinks which he shook like he was strangling a rattlesnake and served gracefully under their noses. Each drink looked like a masterpiece, complete with obligatory umbrellas. Sarah offered a toast. "I know I'm sort of the quiet one of this group, but I feel absolutely effervescent in this hotel and now this restaurant. I'd like to propose a toast to my favorite ladies on the face of this planet, my dear friends

Carla and Joanna. While the rest of our vaunted team aren't here at this moment, I want us to keep them in our thoughts and our prayers. Without each and every one of us contributing, we simply would not be here enjoying this heavenly time and place."

"Here, here," Carla and Joanna said in tandem. "Here's to the best, toughest group of baaad ass women to be found anywhere," added Carla. "Amen sistahs," chirped Joanna. We come, we see, we conquer. *Oohrah*!"

Half way through their drinks, Carla ordered miso soup for all of them and an over the top sushi platter. As they waited for the soup to arrive, Joanna asked the hostess if she could ask the DJ to turn down the volume on the crushing noise, refusing to call it music. "Excuse, me, but that guy is hurting my brain. Would you please tell him it's almost impossible to talk over that cacophony? Ka-caf-phony."

"Over the what?" the hostess, dressed in elegant black with a simple gold pendant and earrings. "The fucking NOISE, you douche bag!"

"Ma'am I'm sorry but we don't appreciate that kind of language in here. And besides, our customers like the… how do you say it… vibe." Joanna smiled as Miss Jerkwad Cuntface walked back to her station.

Joanna let her artist's brain register the noise as only she could. She imagined herself in a steel cocoon, floating on a gentle current in the Caribbean. A gigantic sledgehammer wielded by Zeus pounded on the hull of an aircraft carrier. It looked like the Dwight D. Eisenhower although it was out of station. The sound traveled into her chamber electronically and exploded, she along with it. A tiny trap door opened and oozed out her brain matter, which coagulated and then morphed into her original self. Except it now she was slightly taller and her eyes had turned green to match Carla's. And maybe her American Express card too.

The ladies kept plowing into the visually stunning and drop dead delicious sushi and finally polished it off despite the noise. The ear splitting, brain breaking sound was pure torture. Carla retreated to the ladies room to get some relief while Joanna went back down to the street for a smoke and some decompression. Sarah held their places at the bar and pulled some earplugs out of her purse.

On her way through the lobby, Joanna was impressed with the luxury hotel's extravagant floral arrangements, some of them over five feet tall. Rebirth of a tropical paradise in the middle of a big city. She smiled and nodded at the doorman as she made her way across the street and sat down on the rock wall facing the grand hotel. She lit a cigarillo, inhaled the smoke deep into her lungs and closed her eyes. An old drunk swerved toward her and smelled it. He stood in front of her until she opened her eyes again and without him saying a word, she offered him a smoke. "Please take this and get the fuck away from me. I'm trying to relax here and the sight of you makes me want to puke." The old drunk, he could barely remember his name any more and always had a hard time spelling it, nodded politely and continued to weave down the street, mercifully dragging his stench with him.

Back at the bar at Zuma, Joanna smiled at Carla and kissed her on the cheek. The noise from the DJ was still deafening. Like being under a small metal bridge while tanks crossed overhead tossing grenades out the hatches. The kind of noise that made you want to kill yourself. She approached the hostess again and asked ever so politely if the volume could be turned down a little so they could chat and, heaven forbid, think. "I believe we already had this conversation, Miss…" "Betty. Betty Boop. I'll have to leave you my card before we have to leave this lovely establishment."

Joanna sat back down at the bar and reached into her purse for the small combat knife she always carried. She sauntered over to the DJ and cut his power cords before slicing his throat from ear to ear. The blood gushed down his tropical print shirt, blending beautifully with the crimson flowers. Hostess Jerkwad let out a scream and began to dial 911. Before should could complete the call, Joanna punched the knife through her heart. She found the bug eyed look on her face priceless. Carla and Sarah had anticipated her moves and quickly hustled back down through the lobby, slashing the plants on their way. The doorman was busy flirting with a young blonde with legs up to her tonsils and a perfect tight ass hanging out of her black sequined Corset LBD.

Carla led the way down Boylston Street to the wading pool and then out to Newbury Street where she called for an Uber. The driver, Jose, had been waiting nearby and had them in his back seat in three minutes flat. They headed off to Quincy. They decided to stop at the TJ Maxx, try to blend in a little and pick out some local shmocal outfits, knowing this would be a challenge for them. They met Billy and Freddy there, two guys who were much more hardscrabble and local than they were, being southern belles and all. Carla smeared her makeup off and ditched her jewelry. Joanna and Sarah followed suit and began to browse the isles.

FLAB FESTIVAL

They tried to look at the cheap, make that budget dresses, blouses and jewelry but were distracted by their fellow customers. One drab, grossly overweight woman after another with bad complexions and flabby, age spotted arms. Tattoos, bags under their eyes. Rear ends as wide as a city bus. Carla quickly realized that there was no way they were going to blend in but she mentioned to Joanna what an interesting freak show this was. Sarah thought about speaking up to the effect that it wasn't in God's plan for human beings to be such snobs about each other. She had been at the bottom of the barrel before. Homeless on the street, barely able to scrape together seven dollars for a glass of wine at the bar in Charleston where she met Carla for the first time. She couldn't quite figure out the right words, especially in such a public place. She tried not to frown or look sad but Carla picked up on that immediately. "What's the matter girl, you look like you just swallowed a mouse with rabies or something." "Oh, it's really nothing, I think maybe all the action at Zuma and the fast bumpy ride down here kind of upset my stomach a little. I'll be fine." Billy and Freddy were oblivious to their interaction, choosing to wander over to the men's section and look at shirts that would make them look hip. Their word, hip. They picked out a half a dozen quasi Hawaiians and showed them to Carla and Joanna. "Do you guys like any of these for us? Just don't tell me that would make us look like faggots or something. That's all."

"You fucking homo, Billy," Carla whispered. "You are a fairy. A fucking ugly old senile shit faced fairy." She flashed him that high beam green eyed man killer smile and curtsied. Then burst out laughing and hugged him. Freddie laughed so hard that some of the pukey looking old twats stared at them in mock horror. And the young Serbian or Greek woman with the dark hairy arms. Or maybe it was real horror, nobody seemed to know at that moment. Or care.

Carla walked over to the small furniture collection and found an armchair to relax in. Enough of the homo jokes. She felt embarrassed, but only vaguely. She thought back again of the lovely book called *Eloise* by Kay Thompson that came out before she was born. She had memorized the dust jacket. *"Eloise is a little girl who lives in the Park Plaza Hotel in New York. She is not pretty but she is already a person. She is interested in people when they are not boring. If you take her home with you, you will always be glad you did it."*

Revisiting the 1950s, albeit through the eyes of a fictional girl in a near magical place, it was easy for Carla to envision similar voyages through time. Sometimes she and Sarah liked to listen to music from the 1930s. Glenn Miller was a particular favorite, and the ancient black and white films of young couples dancing to songs like Moonlight Serenade, stars in their young eyes, always seemed to bring tears to theirs. And that got her thinking, amid the dull buzz of TJ Maxx.

What if Mr. Miller's incredible orchestra were to time travel to the present? And listen to some of the best music of today. Maybe whisk them to a Beyoncé concert, or maybe Yo-Yo Ma. How about the Rolling Stones, yeah that's it! With Charlie Watts still alive, of course. He just had to be alive. Lady Gaga, or … oh who knows. What would Miller's boys think about it, what would they say to each other, what would they tell this aging criminal and attorney about their experience?

What if Carla could take them to her favorite tavern afterwards and buy them all drinks so they could really let loose before playing, before their fellow customers of course. She tried to imagine the conversation, Miller's band not quite understanding why they couldn't smoke cigarettes indoors like they always used to back in the day. Marveling at the oddball outfits on some of the women, who often appeared to them like ladies of the night with their skin tight revealing outfits and crazy quilt colored hair. Boobs and asses popping, beckoning.

Flipping the coin over, how about she transported some of today's millennials (forget about twenty somethings) back into a smoky club in the 1930s for a Billie Holiday (Lady Day!) show. Whacha think about them apples, youngsters! No one sings like she did any more, absolutely no one. "Order something to drink if you like and get ready for our next stop which may finish blowing you away."

Millennials in tow, she took a New York subway to another smoky club not far away. On the venue was the incomparable Duke Ellington orchestra. Their next stop was with the one and only Cab Calloway, he of "Minnie the Moocher" and "Blues Brothers" fame. She tried to imagine the fun of introducing him to the kids and then to herself, Joanna, Billy, Freddy, and Sarah. Forget real life, this was a lot more fun.

Before long her young travel mates seemed exhausted and ready to go back to the future. At this point she was a little pooped herself, her mind spinning with the Disneyesque thoughts. Or was it Rod Serling? Hitchcock? Maybe this was an educational experience of a lifetime for everyone involved. Maybe it will get all of them to think outside the box a little bit more about history, culture, and the true joys of human contact floating on a bed of incredible music.

Yeah, that could do the trick, but just thinking about it made her so very tired. She felt suddenly old and desperately needed a nap. But most assuredly it would be a very happy nap. The shopping could wait.

Carla, Sarah, Joanna, Billy and Freddy paid for their new clothes and waited outside the store for their Uber. Billy pulled out a Camel straight. Joanna lit him before putting the Marine Corps Zippo flame to her cigarillo. Store assistant manager hawk nosed pimply Donna Peters came out to ask them to please not smoke so near the entrance. Carla laughed in her face and thanked her from the bottom of her "badass heart" for being such a good worker and her "palpable" concern over public health. Pimples smiled and nodded while she gagged a *fuck you bitch* down her throat. The sixty four grand a year they were paying her just wasn't a goddamn drop in her bucket. Dermatologists and plastic surgeons didn't come free.

Then came a thought, maybe a spark from Joanna's cigarillo that jumped to Carla and the rest. "Hey y'all, let's dump this town for a while and fly to Vegas! Like maybe right now. We can shop for hotshot clothes out there, catch a coupla shows and hit the casinos. Whaddya say? And where should we stay?"

They did some quick online research and came up with Caesars Palace.

VEGAS OR BUST

First, though, full stop. Carla called a meeting between all of them to discuss the gas tank that fueled their efforts and guided their actions. Friendship.

She began the discussion in a secluded location in a nearby park slathered in tall trees and sprinkled with gnomes or whatever the fuck they were and took a long breath before quoting two of the masters. "It is one of the blessings of old friends that you can afford to be stupid with them, **said** Ralph Waldo Emerson. And Mark Twain said Good friends, good books and a sleepy conscience: this is the ideal life. Not bad, eh?"

"You know," continued Carla, "This sort of thing was in the back of my mind when I read a story recently about the great film actress from my youth-- and much earlier-- Leslie Caron. You probably remember her from classics like An American in Paris, Valentino, Daddy Long Legs with Fred Astaire, and yes she was a wonderful dancer, Father Goose with Cary Grant and… wait for it… Gigi with Louis Jourdan and Maurice Chevalier. Among others. Ms. Caron was drop dead lovely to go with all that talent. American audiences loved her. Yet in real life she was painfully shy and often isolated."

She paused just long enough to reinforce their attention. "The article, brilliantly and compassionately written by Simon Hattenstone in The Guardian, drew me right in. If I may quote, Caron is birdlike and as elegant as ever at eighty eight. Her hair is brown and bobbed with the now trademark white streak, eyes large and dusty blue, voice youthful and distinctly French. Her sentences are punctuated with a pealing laugh. From a distance, she sounds so full of joie de vivre. And she is, in a way. But when she tells her story, it is not quite so carefree. In Caron's own words, even as movie star, quote I had a tendency to be melancholy, end quote. Hattenstone also pointed out that during WWII, living in France, young Leslie became anxious and anorexic. Later on, alcoholic and lonely. Yikes, I thought, *the* Leslie Caron?"

Sarah chimed in next. "I read a really cool article by Bill Murphy in Inc., called People Who Embrace These Five Simple Habits Have Very High Emotional Intelligence. Lemme give y'all a hint: people who can honestly answer yes are super poised to make great friends. Are ya ready?

Number one. Do you know how to employ tactical conversational patience? Translated, this means the art of sometimes keeping your mouth closed. Murphy calls it, and this is kinda geeky, calculated unease with a purpose. Most of us, and yep this includes me, have been sort of conditioned to try to fill in conversational gaps. Studying psychology back when didn't undo that for me, but being a mafia kinda girl has, at least to some extent.

Here's another, number two. **Do you learn and practice casual phrases with precise, calculated meanings?'** Here we're talkin' about having a repertoire of go-to phrases so you can avoid saying reflexive and dumb stuff. **So you** replace I'm sorry in your reflexive vocabulary with thanks for understanding. Or, instead of No, I'm busy, you can try thanks for asking, but I'm going to decline. Thank you for understanding. Howdya like them apples?"

Sarah was smoking. "Ok, one more from this guy. Do you always have another question? Murphy says that the most valuable information that we get from interviews usually comes at the end. And therefore, it probably happens in personal conversations as well. Easy peasy, right? OK, ole Murphy gave us a great start on establishing and nurturing terrific friendships. I'd like to offer a few more suggestions, maybe bring us up to an even dozen in total.

For one thing, never and that means EVER do or say something behind your friend's back. Even if they never find out about it, you will have *betrayed a fundamental trust.* And it serves to make you question the very foundation of the relationship. Here's another. And say it like you really mean it. You know, Sally Mae, I would take a bullet for you. At least a verbal one, and put myself at risk in doing so. Our friendship means that much to me."

All eyes were riveted to Sarah. "How 'bout this. Volunteer to do something with this person that you would not ordinarily do or even seriously consider doing. Go with them to the theater, get sweaty with them in their garden, help them cook a special dinner for charity event. Y'all get the idea."

"Yeah, I get it, Sarah-pants," Carla finally chimed back in. "As in, tell them how much they really mean to you. I have a special friend in Cambridge who lives way up in a high rise apartment and we do this regularly. Sure, we like to goof around, go out to dinner and share private thoughts. But I try not to let more than a few days go by without telling her how much I treasure our friendship. No matter where we go or what we do. No exceptions."

"Eggs Ackley," Sarah laughed through her nose in that funky high school dork way of hers. "Like *frequently* ask how they're doing, how they're feeling, what's going on in their lives. None of this how's it going crap. That's just a little too knee-jerk, a little too canned. Some things can well, like tuna. Other things don't. I'm thinking spaghetti. Or clams."

Joanna had finally had enough of the lecture and itched down to her panties to get in the game. "Speaking of clams, don't clam up unless it's absolutely positively necessary with this great friend of yours, or potentially great friend. Try to remember, and this certainly goes for me as well, that wonderful close friendships help make life worth living. As a very special bonus, they may well make your life longer and way more happy. Uh, happier."

Billy finally rose from the dead with Freddy close behind, rubbed his goatee and rasped out a suggestion. "We should definitely hit Vegas all right, but why don't we do some public service first? Like get some of those southern assholes who won't get vaccinated for Covid to maybe change their minds a little. You know, a little gentle persuasion. Or if that don't work..."

Logan Lessons

Carla jumped on the idea.

Carla "String Bean" D'Andrea, Billy O'Connell and their gang headed to Logan Airport fully loaded. They planned to get heavier weapons once they got to Beaufort, South Carolina, where they were easy to obtain, but in the meantime felt secure with 3-D printed hand guns. Plastic, no serial numbers, and they usually won't show up on airport scanners. It was Friday night so Logan was packed as usual, virtually everyone wearing masks against Covid infection. They grabbed meatball with provolone sandwiches along with a few beers and headed to the gate. As usual, men's necks could be heard cracking as they stared at Carla strolling along.

Their flight was pleasantly uneventful, punctuated by cocktails and idle chatter. The flight attendants were cheerful and even cracked a few jokes with them. Billy reeled off a few off golden oldies from Jack Benny back in the twelfth century. Okay, the 1950's. Whatever. Somehow they were still funny, or at least the flight crew was well trained enough to go along with it. Carla frankly didn't give a shit either way. Benny was before her time anyway. They switched planes in Charlotte, North Carolina and the wait for once was short. They noticed how modern, even elegant this airport was. Fancy shops in a quasi-mall configuration. Even the news stand was pretty cool, run by a little Chinese dude. They picked up a couple copies of the Charlotte Observer, Charleston Post and Courier, and even found a small stack of the Beaufort Gazette. It felt good holding actual newspapers in their hands and not having to get everything off their phones. That was kid stuff. Fuck kids. Especially the unvaccinated Republican ones, which was most of them down here. Just fuck 'em.

The flight into the Beaufort Executive Airport was a crisp one hour and ten minutes. Nothing much else to do so they read their papers and dozed off, Billy falling first with a power saw snore that made a half dozen of his fellow passengers laugh out loud.

Little Lizbeth Carter so hard that her chocolate milk squirted out of her nose, forcing her mother to chase down a Kleenex. Then another. Mr. Carter was oblivious. He had seen the milk movie before. His main objective was to keep the slop off his new suit. His word, slop.

Carla's Southern Ladies Mafia and Billy's Boston Boppers deplaned in Beaufort County, former home of the one and only Pat Conroy, took an Uber to Rhett House in downtown Beaufort and checked in. Joanna couldn't resist breaking into song at the beautiful place's name. Jimmy Hendrix came to her mind, circa 1966.

"There's a red house over yonder
That's where my baby stays
Lord, there's a red house over yonder
Lord, that's where my baby stays
Wait a minute something's wrong here,
The key won't unlock this door
Wait a minute, something's wrong

"Sing that thang, girl," Carla said.

"Shit you were just a little bittie, not even a tween in the sixties," Billy lectured. I was there, you young twerp. Freddy and me even saw him play. Holy fucking shit, remember Freddy?"

"Man, that's not the kind of thing you forget. Now let's check out our rooms, *yawl*! Did I say that right?"

Located on Craven Street in Beaufort's northwest quadrant, an easy walk south from Pigeon Point, Rhett House oozed southern charm and elegance. The rooms stately yet somehow understated, a treat for the eyes and a heavenly respite for the weary. Mouthwatering breakfasts were offered every day and included in the price. Carla, Joanna, Sarah, Billy and Freddy settled in like cats in front of a fireplace. After a short nap, they met on the huge second-floor balcony and drank in every luscious detail. Freddy passed a joint around. Called it medical. For the rest of the day they planned their attack on Covid vaccine holdouts. Anti-vaxers. They were determined to play nice, for a while.

First stop the next morning, after a huge breakfast of fresh fruit, eggs, toast and the obligatory grits was Dataw Island, a private gated community featuring two eighteen hole golf courses. They couldn't just waltz in unannounced, so relied on Carla's friend and longtime island resident, Pat Shields to phone the guard shack. When they got there in their rented van, Guard Sommers waved them through.

None of them had ever been to Dataw, but they had done some online research and if anything it was lovelier than the photos they had seen. Manicured lawns, live oak and palmetto trees everywhere, even some tall pines. Hawks here and there and even a few bald eagles. Bald fucking eagles for crissake. Freddy and Billy almost felt at home staring at those pines. They passed the stately clubhouse with its regal entrance after getting a quick look at the public garden. A huge orange tree, heavy with fruit, caught their attention along with the perfectly tended individual plots.

DOWN PAT

Once at Pat's home, a four bedroom pastel yellow masterpiece overlooking the Morgan River, they were greeted with that famous southern hospitality. "Well hey, y'all, welcome to our little community! Let me give you a quick tour of the grounds and maybe then we can have some coffee out on the porch. I've got regular and decaf all set to go, and there's some fresh Dunkin donuts around here someplace and I've even got coconut but I'll bet y'all already had a huge breakfast at Rhett House. M'I right?"

"Yes, actually we did but some decaf sounds nice," Carla responded. "Wow, look at all those hydrangeas, did you plant those yourself? And is that a lemon tree over there?"

"Yep and double yep. Thanks for noticing. And those over there are Firecracker Plants, Shadbush, and Eastern Bluestar. Y'all like 'em?"

"Good golly Miss Molly," Joanna said. "I could stay here and paint for days. We don't really have these where I come from, you know, Boston and thereabouts. Wish I'd brought some of my gear and some paint."

"Oh don't you worry about that, any friend of Carla's is a friend of mine and you can come back here anytime. Plus we can fetch you all kinda paints and such."

Up on the porch with decafs all around, Carla eased into a gentle discussion of Covid and southerners' frequent reluctance to just get their stupid asses vaccinated.

Pat quickly took the bait. "You know, I'm not much of a social media gal, and neither is my husband Harry. He's out playing golf by the way, probably be back in a couple hours. You'll like him. But I was reading this fellow Juan Williams talk about how the big social media companies like that damned Facebook are really letting us all down. Like big time, you know?

He talked about a report from the nonprofit Center for Countering Digital Hate on the Disinformation Dozen. They've got this list that shows only a dozen people could be responsible for sharing two thirds of all the anti-vaccine bullshit on social media. Excuse my language, let's just say garbage. And Facebook hasn't done a thing to stop this crap. Can I say crap here everybody?"

"Darn tootin," answered Billy. "Amen," added Sarah.

"And if I may sorta quote this Juan Willams," Pat continued. "Talk about gas lighting, or disorienting people by talking about side issues to distract them from the big truth. Yes, there is good information on Facebook and lots of people like it. Millions. But the far more pivotal fact is the load of bad information on Facebook."

"I guess the real question is how do we get all these Republican crackers and farmers and nuts and stupidos to just shut the hell up and get their shots," Carla continued. "To hell with their so called freedoms. They're not free to make other people sick. And weren't they pretty much all vaccinated against polio as kids? I mean it's safe, works extremely well, and free. And no it won't make women infertile, though what exactly would be wrong with that with these bozos, or magnetic or really sick. Or the vaccine enters your cells and changes your DNA, that's a beauty. Or *causes* Covid or whatever other bogus excuses people come up with. What a giant stinking pot of *bullshit*. And these morons are holding back the economy for Pete's sake and *killing* people."

A pissed off, sweaty old golfer trudged up the steps to the porch. It was Harry Shields, back early after a miserable nine holes. All six foot one of him, still sporting those IBM blue eyes Pat fell for thirty-five years ago.

"Hi, sweetie, back so soon? Were the bugs out there today?"

"I didn't see any no-see-ums, if that's what you mean. But I just kept shanking shots I normally crush and then my danged back started to hurt. So I gave up the ghost."

"Well, that sounds just awful, but you'll be fine tomorrow. Here, why don't you join us. This is my old friend Carla D'Andrea. She used to practice law at a hotshot firm in Charleston. And these are her traveling companions… Joanna, Sarah, Billy and Freddy. Hey you guys, meet the greatest husband in South Carolina."

"South Carolina my butt, how about the entire east coast of the USA, baby."

"Sure, young man, you got it! Now how about joining us in our fascinating discussion of why so many folks out there just refuse to get vaccinated for Covid. Didn't you read some ideas from a psychologist or something? What was her name?"

"Peggy Drexler. Yeah, she's a psychologist, kind of like your nephew Jake. A research psychologist, she's also a documentary producer and published a bunch of stuff. She got interviewed by CNN after the delta variant lit the country on fire. Cases way up. Hospitalizations. Deaths for crissake. She admitted that some of these bozos are hard to deal with, but she had a few suggestions."

"Care to share them with us baby boy?"

"Sure, sweetie. One thing she said was Listen. Vaccine resistance is complicated and based in a tangled web of beliefs and emotions. Some people are scared of side effects. Or they're mad at our government, or maybe China, for quote *forcing* them to get the shot in the first place. She suggested that we not get all pumped up trying to bombard them with data and facts or the little fairies might feel attacked. That you gotta listen patiently to their individual concerns and fears.

She also suggested that you **talk in way that will help them listen**. She called it quote charm and disarm. You know, like appeal—that was her word, appeal-- to their softer side, and their fondness for you, by making it personal. I think that was a direct quote. And explain why the vaccine is personally important to you. Like in an effort to help save your own family, or friends and neighbors. Co-workers. Like that.

She also mentioned, and I really love this one with those morons, stay detached. Don't shame them or scold them, and don't get openly pissed off. Excuse my French. Irritated. Make them feel safe around you or some such thing. Safe, yeah that was it. Freaking safe. Like you're the boogeyman. And the last thing I remember from this interview was she said it's okay to offer them a bribe. Lunch or something. Can you believe that stuff?"

Refreshed and energized from their porch chat and coffee, Carla and her gang said goodbye to Pat and Harry and headed back to Beaufort's Rhett House. After a brief nap they reconvened on the balcony and plotted their next moves.

"How about we meander into the emergency room at Beaufort Memorial Hospital and sort of check things out. See how many Covid patients are there, talk to the staff, charm some of the docs and nurses. Get my drift kids? What say?"

"Yeah, I like that," Billy replied. "Maybe they can check out this hammer toe of mine and tell me if I have shingles. I've been itching and aching for days now and never got that shingles vaccine they've got."

"Hammer *toe*?" mocked Joanna. "How about hammer *head* and brass balls that turned into lead lately, you old meathead."

"I'll take that as a ringing endorsement, Ms. Ciampa. So let's do it. Where's our driver anyway?"

Sarah jumped on her iPhone and had a private limo service there in fifteen minutes. The driver, Eduardo, tall and gently off-handsome if a little too swarthy for some folks, took an immediate shine to the three lovely ladies. "Hey everybody, I'm here and rarin' to go. Sarah said something about running over to the hospital."

"You got it, Eddy. Ok everyone, jump in. He may look like a pimp or something but I can vouch for him from back in my homeless days. He used to pity me on the streets in Charleston and bring me food and girl supplies once in a while and he always had that suave Latin thing going on."

All the way to the hospital, Sarah began to lose it. She felt snakes in her stomach. Not the cute kind, but sea snakes. Ugly ones that fueled her paranoia. She felt one come up through her mouth and bit down hard. It tasted like rubber cement or that gooey crap they were always blabbering about on cable TV, Flex Seal. She had never actually eaten that stuff, who would ever do that, but this snake sure tasted like that stuff would. She bit its head off and spit it out the window. It glanced off the sidewalk and smiled at her, taunted her, telling her they were plenty more coming up her throat. Sarah felt her spine vibrating. It felt cold and hostile. Maybe going to the emergency room would be a good idea after all. She could puke all over and fit right in.

Eddy pulled up to 955 Ribaut Road. They had arrived at the modest hospital with limited parking for visitors. The air was bright and crinkly. The sky was smoky blue, the trees in the parking lot blending right in. Fully armed, and as dangerous as ever, they walked into the waiting room and sat down. Billy went over to the vending machine and got some M&M's for himself and a small bag of peanuts for Freddy. The ladies said they would pass for now. They had business to do.

The hospital waiting room looked like somebody had come in with a stiff brush and new mop and it smelled like it had just been polished. Lemony fresh. A grossly overweight black woman sat behind the reception desk calling patients up one at a time to sign in. Carla took the lead.

"Good afternoon, Mabel. That's such a pretty name. My mother's name was Mabel too. I need to see a doctor pretty quick. I've been having heart palpitations and sweating even indoors. I have a chronic heart condition so I'm scared. How fast do you think someone can see me?" Mabel looked up from her desk bored as a soggy shingle after a hurricane.

"Just use that monitor over there to sign yourself in. We're running pretty good right now so someone should be able to grab you in five minutes or so. Are those other four people with you?"

"Yeah, they're with me. They're in trouble too but we decided I should go first on account of my heart and all. I'll just sit back down and tell them what you said. Thank you for being so kind, and I love your hair."

The first man Carla approached was an 80-year-old white guy with canyon wrinkles and grape tomato sized age spots. He wore baggy blue jeans, white sneakers as old as he was, and a powder blue short sleeve shirt. Anchor tattoos bled from his left forearm. At least she thought they were anchors. They could've been almost anything. Maybe they were boogers. Or rat turds. He smelled like whiskey and popcorn. Eyes like black tunnels.

"Good afternoon sir, my name is Carla. I'm from Charleston. I work up there at a douche bag law firm when I'm not robbing banks. What brings you here if I might ask? By the way, you look like hell and I'm wondering if you've been vaccinated against the virus. Pardon me if I'm being too personal but my friends and I are on a sort of mission from God."

"Ralph. Ralph Buckley. Goddamn you're pretty. I bet you get that all the time. And no I ain't been vaccinated. Don't have a taste for it, but I sure would like to taste your pussy."

Joanna heard every word. Like a rat with its ass on fire, she went over to Ralph and gave him a monster karate chop to the neck. His head snapped back as blood squirted from his nose and mouth. If it was humanly possible, he looked worse than he did before she hit him. Her boss was not happy and grabbed her shoulder. "You cunt, what did you do that for? That bitch at the counter is going to call security and we are *cooked*. Grab the others and head down the street. Make a right. There's a Piggly Wiggly down there then we can hang out for a few minutes. You're lucky I don't poke your eyes out, bitch. Go on now, move your ass."

PIG OUT

Duly rebuked, Joanna rounded up Billy, Freddy and Sarah and they skated out the door. Piggly Wiggly sounded like a good place to hang out for a while. They had a decent salad bar and the bananas were always fresh. No spots. No fruit flies. Usually.

The Pig was a five minute walk down Ribaut Road. Nestled in a dingy shopping center next to a liquor store and a hardware joint with a decent bowling alley close by across the street, it was the perfect place to hide out for a few minutes. Maybe the security guys wouldn't find them. That was the plan anyway. Stay away from those fucking security guys, for their sake anyway. They were all fully armed and ready for anything. But why pick a fight when you didn't have to. Even Billy agreed with that, though Freddy wasn't quite so sure.

Piggly Wiggly was the typical South Carolina supermarket. Squat black women roaming the isles and checking out with bored white girls. Same old stuff every day. But for Carla's purposes, it meant predictability. She had been in the store several times before. Usually to pick up fruit and occasionally a salad. The food was decent enough, just plain. Plain as cold oatmeal on a paper plate. But it wouldn't kill you. Not right away usually. Food poisoning maybe.

They grabbed some bananas, strawberries, and what they were told was grits with raisins. It looked like vomit. The kind those people in the emergency room would churn up. They paid in cash as usual and made their way out into the parking lot. Billy snagged a six pack of Rolling Rock beer from the adjacent liquor store and sat down in a huff. Freddy lit a joint, leaned back and smiled at the sun. "OK team, drink up. That emergency room thing was a bust. Thanks to you, Joanna. You just had to clock that guy, didn't you? You could've smacked him in the nose gently to get his attention but no, you had to really hurt the guy and probably get hospital security down on our asses. Nice work, sweetheart. Here, is this chilled enough for you? You cold hearted bitch." She smiled that gorgeous brown eyed smile of hers and he grinned right back, reaching out for a bear hug. They laughed like kids at a picnic.

A fat assed white woman, about thirty five, walked out the door. She was wearing a midriff blouse and all her flab was hanging out. All up and down her arms and neck were disgusting tattoos. Sleeves. Barf. She looked like a slut on cocaine, a fat stupid slut. Freddy was ready to throw up. She was ruining his buzz. Joanna handed him a paper bag and told him to keep it together. They had to remain low key and off the radar. It was no time for theatrics. Or puking.

Another white woman followed the fat bag of shit out the door. She was gorgeous. Five foot nine, natural blonde, with just a tantalizing hint of blonde peach fuzz on her arms. Billy got a hard on and Carla smacked him in the balls. "Hey what the fuck? Can't I just enjoy the scenery once in a while with you?"

"You piece of shit, no, no, and no. Keep your boner to yourself for once."

She wasn't finished with him. "Enjoy the scenery somewhere else you shithead. You're with three gorgeous girls, and you're getting a hard on with that slut that just walked out of the market. OK, she was pretty, unlike the other turds in there. But we're here on business, OK? Alright look, see those guys coming out now? See if they've been vaccinated. Make nice with them."

The three guys looked old as sand. Shabby, probably penniless after buying groceries. All skinny and crabbed over. Dressed like shit on a fucking shingle.

Billy walked over to the men and introduced himself. "Hi, my name is Orlando Davis. I'm a nurse over at the hospital and I was just wondering if I could ask you gentlemen a few questions."

"Yeah, like what?" said the one in the middle.

"Well for one thing, where did you get that shirt? I really like it. And also, I'm curious if you've been vaccinated yet."

"Well, TJ Maxx as a matter fact and no way. What business is it of yours? Are you really a nurse? You look like a washed up piece of donkey crap. Excuse my French."

Billy reached into his pocket and pulled out a Covid shot. As he approached the man, he spooked and pivoted. Billy tried to grab his arm and missed. On his second try, the syringe went into the man's nose. The guy screamed and started bleeding. Billy apologized and looked at Carla. She said "nice work you moron," and got on her phone. Three minutes later, their driver Eduardo was on the scene and the five of them jumped in the car. "Get us the fuck out of here. Now. Take us somewhere safe. Like back to Dataw."

PEACE AND QUIET AND OPEN AIR

Eddie drove back to Dataw Island, smooth as Wesson oil on a hot George Foreman grill, straight to Pat's place. They pulled up and parked in the pebbled circular driveway. They walked up to the porch and before they could knock, Pat came through the screen door and welcomed them back. "Hey you guys, what a nice surprise. Can you stay for a while? Harry's in there mixing a pitcher of margaritas. Should I tell him to bring out glasses for everyone?"

"Yeah, that would be just great," said Carla. We are kind of thirsty. Had a bit of an altercation at the hospital and down at the Piggly Wiggly too. Billy here started the whole thing but he's very sorry. Aren't you Billy?"

"Yeah, right kiddo. I'm sooo very sorry. Sad Sack sorry. Little kid who shit the bed sorry. You bet."

Harry came out a few minutes later with a pitcher of margaritas. It quickly sweat up a storm with the afternoon humidity, tears dribbling down. He knew instinctively to go back in the house for some munchies. He came out with a loaded silver tray. Joanna eyed it hungrily. Triscuits, hummus, clam dip, Gouda cheese slices, and a huge wedge of aged cheddar. Freddy was starving. He stuck his finger in the clam dip and Carla karate chopped him in the neck.

"What the hell did you do that for?" Freddy wailed.

"We're guests here, you old fool. I'm sorry, Pat, he gets a little rambunctious sometimes. And Harry, these margaritas are great. What kind of tequila do you use?"

"Don Julio today. Sometimes Jose Cuervo. I don't really think Pat can tell the difference but I like the Don Julio better. At least I think I do. I got that Gouda cheese at the Big Y last week. They had it on sale doncha know. Also that cheddar wedge. And guess what?

I went out clamming with my buddy Roger and we did pretty well with the clams. So I can vouch for the fact that we worked for every darn one of them and they're really fresh."

The conversation turned back to the pandemic and why so many people were holding out on getting the vaccine. "So what's going on, Pat and Harry, in the good old south?" Carla mused. "I hope I'm not repeating myself but why are so many people not getting the Covid shot? I mean we just came down from Boston and most people up there have enough common sense to just get the damn shot. But here in South Carolina? Different story. And what about Alabama, Mississippi, Louisiana and all those Republican states around the country. What the hell is wrong with those people? Are they just being selfish or stupid or both?"

Pat jumped right in. "Well it's a little more complicated than that, especially in the south. People don't generally get their news from good reliable sources like the Washington Post, the New York Times, Washington Post, Bloomberg, Reuters, CNN or maybe the BBC. They get their news from Fox and listen to morons, make that greedy *morons* like Tucker Carlson, Laura Ingraham and that stinking selfish pig Sean Hannity. And of course they go on social media and wallow in just an endless stream of garbage. Facebook is pretty bad but there's much worse, believe it or not.

Excuse my language, not necessarily garbage, I should say conspiracy theories. Like the vaccine will make you magnetic, or infertile, or, then here's one of my favorites. The vaccine has got these secret little chips in them from the Chinese or something so they can track you wherever you go and get all your personal information. I know that sounds crazy, but that's what these people are listening to. Personally, I don't think Tucker Carlson is particularly stupid. I think he's playing to the crowd, the home field. He's greedy for ratings which makes his wallet thicker. And apparently he's got no conscience about spreading baloney. Notice I didn't say bullshit."

Carla and Billy stood up and kissed their hostess. "Pat, we need to stretch out and go for a walk. We'll be back in a little while." They were wobbly drunk and stuffed from all the food. And ready for action.

Billy grabbed his satchel and off they went. Straight for the club. It was only about two miles away and the walk did them good. They arrived at the plush, cushy pavilion Republican middle-class entitlement bastion in fifteen minutes. Walked slowly up the steps hand-in-hand. Looking like fathers and daughters to anyone who was paying any attention.

Pat had called ahead for them. They were warmly greeted and seated overlooking the Morgan River. The view was spectacular with the sun bleeding down in the west. Everything was crisp and fresh as roasted cashews. They ordered Heineken's and stared at each other. "Well kiddos, are you ready to rock 'n' roll?" asked Billy.

"Yeah dude, like always," Carla answered. "I'm going to try to charm the pants off some of these old fucker men and find out if they've been vaccinated. You stay here and take notes. Then get ready to rumble."

Carla made the rounds alright. She flashed those lightning green eyes at a dozen men and introduced herself as Betty Grable. Actually her granddaughter. Wide eyed white haired man felt their necks creaking as they bowed to her charms. Most of their wives looked on with bemusement. There he goes again. I think he's getting a hard on. Maybe he'll save it for me for later. Carla signaled Billy with recon on their vaccination status. Billy was drunk, but not that drunk. He joined her and pulled out his satchel. They went table to table stabbing old white Republican men in the arm with the Moderno vaccine. Most of the patrons actually stopped watching the golf channel and looked on in horror. Goddamn gob smacked. Chip Williams Junior took out his iPhone and called 911. Three squad cars arrived in 10 minutes. The six officers walked up the steps and entered the club. Three white guys, three black. They did not look happy.

It took them 30 seconds to locate Carla and her gang. Fortunately for her, she had packed a semi-automatic pistol in her purse. Naturally, she had to open fire. Four of the officers fell flat on her faces. The other two crashed onto a few of the other diners' tables. The club smelled like smoke, beer, and chaos. Another day at the office for Carla D'Andrea.

Carla and Billy, two badass desperados, went to the rest rooms and donned plastic masks they had ordered online. "Hmm, not bad" Carla said into the mirror. "Not bad at all." On their way out the door, they threw a fire bomb behind them. In seconds, the club was an inferno. They laughed as they walked out the driveway and headed back toward Pat's house. "Well, we did it again Billy boy," Carla said. "We fucking did it again you old piece of shit."

After giving Pat and Harry huge wet kisses, the five of them got into an Uber X van and headed for Augusta, Georgia. They still had business to do. They were on a mission from God. And the devil.

GEORGIA ON THEIR MINDS

The cab got them to the Marriott on James Brown Boulevard in three hours. Most of them slept on the way. But not Carla. She was the boss, the ringleader. The woman with the electric green eyes. All powerful, all knowing. All trouble. A god damned sociopath and she knew it. Tough shit everybody. Nobody's perfect. Who are you to sit there and judge me, you ugly cunt faced bitch.

They checked in, all polite and smiley. Their rooms were pleasant but this sure wasn't the Four Seasons. She slipped into a robe and slippers and put her feet up. Her brain traveled to a distant place. A very long way off.

There was so much more to learn about time travel. Was it really just a fantasy, or did modern physics support the idea? What did Einstein say about it? What about Stephen Hawking? She pondered an article she had read in Science Borealis. Indeed, she had practically memorized parts of it. The article was written by Chenoa van den Boogaard, their physics and astronomy editor. It was entitled "Time Travel Is Possible, But It's A One-Way Ticket."

The article began simply enough. *"Real-life time travel occurs through time dilation, a property of Einstein's special relativity. Einstein was the first to realize that time is not constant, as previously believed, but instead slows down as you move faster through space."*

As she recalled, as part of his theory, Einstein re-imagined space itself. He coined the term "spacetime," fusing the three dimensions of space and one dimension of time into a single term. Rather than treating space as a flat and rigid place that holds all the objects in the universe, Einstein believed it was curved and malleable, able to form gravitational dips around masses that pull other objects in, just as a bowling ball placed in the center of a trampoline would cause any smaller object placed on the trampoline to slide towards the center.

The next part of the article she recalled dead on. *"The closer an object gets to the center of the dip, the faster it accelerates. The center of the Earth's gravitational dip is located at the Earth's core, where gravitational acceleration is strongest. According to Einstein's theory, because time moves more slowly as you move faster through space, the closer an object is to the center of the Earth, the slower time moves for that object.*

This effect can be seen in GPS satellites, which orbit 20,200 kilometers above the Earth's surface. These satellites have highly precise clocks onboard that gain an average of 38 microseconds per day due to time dilation. While this time gain seems insignificant, GPS satellites rely on their onboard clocks to maintain precise global positioning. Running 38 microseconds fast would result in a positioning error of nearly 10 kilometers, an error that would increase daily if the time difference were not constantly corrected.

A more dramatic example of time dilation can be seen in the movie Interstellar *when Matthew McConaughey and his crew land on a planet with an extreme gravitational field caused by a nearby black hole. Because of the black hole's intense gravitational influence, time slows dramatically for the crew on the planet, making one hour on the surface equal to seven years on Earth. This is why, when the crew returns to Earth, Matthew McConaughey's daughter is an old woman while he appears to be the same age as when he left."*

Carla's legal mind was still a steel trap. As she recalled from the article, while it would be pretty dang cool to travel back in time to encounter some dinosaurs or to meet Albert Einstein and show him the reality of time travel, maybe it would be preferable if the past stayed untouched. Travelling back in time invites the potential for making a change that could destroy the future. Like in *Back to the Future*, Marty McFly travels to the past and unwittingly prevents his parents from meeting each other, nearly preventing his own existence.

In a study conducted at the University of Queensland, the researchers proved mathematically that paradox-free time travel is possible, thereby showing that the universe will self-correct to avoid inconsistencies. If this is right, then even if we could travel back in time, we would never be able to jiggle events to create a different future. Stephen Hawking had a great line here. *"The best evidence we have that time travel into the past is not possible, and never will be, is that we have not been invaded by hordes of tourists from the future."*

At long last, the rest of Carla's team was getting bored. They could make only so many trips to the Morris Museum, a trivially easy walk from the hotel to the River Walk. They had seen all the exhibitions. Manning Wilson. The Murphys of Savannah. Linda Fantuzzo. Jack Island Trials. They had wandered the amazing bakery across from the hotel and all the local restaurants, and there were plenty.

After three nights in Georgia, the routine got stale as last month's daily paper. It was time to head back to South Carolina, to Pat and Harry's comfortable home on Dataw Island. They packed quickly, snagged a comfortable ride with their pal Eddy, and arrived in three hours with light traffic. Billy gazed out the back window at the birds and local critters. The rest of them slept while he pondered the heavens. And starlight. He thought about Ellen Farber, the only woman he had ever really loved, the kind of love that staples your soul to your heart. He recalled a passage in the great Dennis Lehane's book Mystic River.

"Brendan Harris loved Katie Marcus like crazy, loved her like movie love, with an orchestra booming through his blood and flooding his ears. He loved her waking up, going to bed, loved her all day and every second in between. Brendan Harris would love Katie Marcus fat and ugly. He'd love her with bad skin and no breasts and thick fuzz on her upper lip. He'd love her toothless. He'd love her bald."

On his way to see his Ellen in Cambridge one afternoon, she was loitering at the hair salon, being done up by the owner, Betty. Billy relaxed in a comfortable chair behind her and watched the two of them work their magic. He thought about the lovely private garden next-door. The first thing he noticed was the wind chimes. There was just enough breeze to keep them jingling. A small sign in the garden said "gardening is lovesome." He wondered who could argue with that. A young father walked by with his two darling girls in tow wearing pink sneakers. Oh my goodness, he thought, how cute!

As Ellen and Betty finished at the salon, he thought back to an old Julie Andrews song written by Rogers and Hammerstein. He thought the lyrics would be as beautiful in fifty years as they were today.

Raindrops on roses and whiskers on kittens
Bright copper kettles and warm woolen mittens
Brown paper packages tied up with strings
These are a few of my favorite things.

Cream-colored ponies and crisp apple strudels;
Doorbells and sleigh bells and schnitzel with noodles;
Wild geese that fly with the moon on their wings;

Maybe it just took him this long to finally realize that life is just too damn short to stay miserable. There's just too much runway ahead and way too much starlight.

CODE RED

Carla rocked back-and-forth on Pat's porch and looked around at her comrades. Maybe they had this rampage thing all wrong. Maybe they were heading for jail. And just maybe they all deserved it.

She thought back on her time growing up in Charleston. A terribly pretty, long legged girl with an aggressive streak but fluid enough to charm the pants off a statue of Robert E. Lee. Almost everyone loved her, even most of her teachers who often found her somewhat rebellious and extremely willful. Those green eyes of Carla's were a weapon. She knew that from the age of ten. By age thirteen or so, some of the boys climaxed in front of her on sight. Embarrassed, they ran for the bathrooms. Carla always got a kick out of that, the power of it all.

The sun began to arc toward the sea. Spanish moss on the live oak trees in Pat's front yard waved to her, seeming to anticipate her next move. A hawk landed on one, clutching a mouse. The poor little guy never stood a chance. Like most of Carla's victims over the years.

A wistful young man named Henry Baskin once spotted her sprouting manic if not psychopathic tendencies. He had fallen in love with her against his better judgement. In desperation, he wrote a poem for her.

Angel with Her Wings On Fire

There soars a young woman
Who lives in my heart
Animates my soul
Spirit
Existence.
An angel from another planet

Too much for poor Earth.
She flies much too high
Too fast
Too far.
Hard to live with her
Impossible without.
Desperate and hungry
She feeds on my love.
Then flies off too high
Too fast
Much too far
Burnt feathers fall on my shoulders.

Carla had long thought about her potential personality disorder. Make that probable. The terms psychopath and sociopath always came to mind, even though she knew that doctors, actually shrinks, didn't usually use those terms. They seemed to prefer the more antiseptic term antisocial personality disorder. Mostly these people seemed to have trouble distinguishing right and wrong, or so she heard.

Apparently a psychopath flat out lacks a conscience. If she lies to someone so she can grab their money, she won't exactly experience any moral calamity, though she might fake it. Yeah baby, fake it till you make it. A sociopath supposedly has a weak conscience, whatever that meant. Maybe they know that stealing your money is wrong and they might even feel a smidge of guilt but they'll do it any way.

Carla learned that both types aren't exactly strong on empathy. They have trouble putting themselves in someone else's place and figure out how they might feel. Ah, tough shit. And what the fuck do shrinks know anyway.

The sun began to arc toward the sea. Spanish moss on the live oak trees in Pat's front yard waved to her, seeming to anticipate her next move. A hawk landed on one, clutching a mouse. The poor little guy never stood a chance. Like most of Carla's victims over the years.

A South Carolina state police car crunched up the driveway. Out came two huge troopers, bulging at the seams. One white, one black. Each well over six feet tall. They did not look happy. The white guy looked around and said, "Which one of you is Carla?"

The hawk looked on and smiled. She saw everything.